LOCKDOWN

MAGGIE BOLITHO

Great Plains Teen Fiction
(an imprint of Great Plains Publications)
233 Garfield Street
Winnipeg, MB R3G 2M1
www.greatplains.mb.ca

Great Plains Publications gratefully acknowledges the financial support provided for its publishing program by the Government of Canada through the Canada Book Fund; the Canada Council for the Arts; the Province of Manitoba through the Book Publishing Tax Credit and the Book Publisher Marketing Assistance Program; and the Manitoba Arts Council.

Design & Typography by Relish Design Studio Inc.
Printed in Canada by Friesens

Library and Archives Canada Cataloguing in Publication

Bolitho, Maggie, author
    Lockdown / Maggie Bolitho.

Issued in print and electronic formats.
ISBN 978-1-926531-89-2 (pbk.).--ISBN 978-1-926531-90-8 (epub).--
ISBN 978-1-926531-91-5 (mobi)

    I. Title.

PS8603.O4597L62 2014   jC813'.6   C2013-908735-4
                                                C2013-908736-2

ENVIRONMENTAL BENEFITS STATEMENT

Great Plains Publications saved the following resources by printing the pages of this book on chlorine free paper made with 100% post-consumer waste.

TREES	WATER	ENERGY	SOLID WASTE	GREENHOUSE GASES
8	3,724	4	249	687
FULLY GROWN	GALLONS	MILLION BTUs	POUNDS	POUNDS

Environmental impact estimates were made using the Environmental Paper Network Paper Calculator 3.2. For more information visit www.papercalculator.org.

FSC
www.fsc.org
MIX
Paper from
responsible sources
FSC® C016245

To Alan Bolitho, with love

CHAPTER 1 | QUAKE

NORTH VANCOUVER

"The enemy's catching up, Oliver—run!" I glanced down at him and he wagged his tail. Half wire-haired terrier, half Mexican jumping bean, he looked like a metal scouring pad on long skinny legs. My little cartoon buddy.

Behind us, my brother, Michael, and the gum-chewing kid from next door, trampled like a herd of spooked wildebeests. They couldn't sneak up on a dead girl, let alone me.

"Rowan! Where the hell are you?" called Michael, four years older than me and a total control freak. Was I so hard to see? Almost six feet tall with a thick mane of brown hair, I didn't exactly fade into the background.

I ran faster and Oliver loped beside me. I'd been running all summer, mostly away from my father, Tony. Once we were really close, but lately we couldn't breathe the same air without a fight breaking out. He gave me his opinion on every single thing I did and never listened to my ideas about anything. I was nearly sixteen freaking years old and swimming in quicksand. The more I struggled to be free of him, the more he demanded to know where I was every minute. When he wasn't near me in person, he made Michael his spy. Five minutes late and it was battle stations, everyone.

Whenever I could, I broke free to the forest. It was only a fifteen-minute walk from Tony's house, but it was a different world. A private kingdom with nothing between me and Alaska but mountains and forest. If I got lost, I could follow the creeks back to the ocean and North Vancouver's rocky beaches. But I never did. Not even when I took the unmarked trails that the tourists and day-trippers didn't know.

Today Michael decided to join me, and wherever he went, Jake went too. Jake was Michael's good deed for the week. Jake didn't like being in the house alone when his mom was away overnight so he became our guest. Even though he was a little older than me, he seemed way younger, so I kept my distance.

I speeded up and Oliver followed. A small brown squirrel darted into the middle of the path and shot up a nearby tree. Oliver tore after it. He barked frantically and danced on his hind legs.

"Zeeta!" I used our special word from obedience training. The emergency recall command worked its magic. Oliver ran to my side and claimed his treat.

The squirrel perched on a low branch and chirped a distress call that sounded like a dying smoke detector. Then it was gone. Oliver and I started running again, fleeing the evil shadows before they caught us.

We plunged deeper into the woods.

The light rain, which had been falling since morning, stopped. A suffocating blanket of air hung heavy and humid over everything. I could barely breathe.

An eerie silence descended around me, and I didn't want to be alone. I clenched and unclenched my fists. The forest felt strange, foreign. Oliver whined for reassurance but I didn't have any to spare, so I slipped him another treat instead. When Michael and Jake hauled themselves up the hill behind us, I finally exhaled.

"Thought you were going for a walk, not a bloody race," Michael said in his usual charming way. Even though he's way older than me, we look a lot alike. His hair was frizzy from the rain and I knew mine was way worse.

My bangs curled and stuck together so when I flicked them slightly, they moved in a single lump. "Oliver went after a squirrel."

"You'd better not let him go after a skunk." Michael glared at Oliver as if he had done something wrong. "Tony'll have a meltdown if he comes home reeking again."

"Why d'you think I spent *months* teaching him emergency recalls?" Trust Michael to act like a tool when he should have been congratulating me. It was the middle of August and not a single skunk incident this year. "Besides Oliver was perfect; he came back right away."

Oliver didn't act proud or happy. His envelope-flap ears lay flat against his head and he stared into the forest. Then he growled low and deep. He was spooking me and I wished he'd stop.

"Sit!" Jake said in a nervous singsong tone that made my back teeth ache. Why'd he come anyway? If his mom knew he was in Lynn Canyon Park she'd have a hissy fit. She'd act like he'd flown to Mexico to make a drug deal, not walked a couple of blocks to a public park.

"Dogs like high-pitches," Jake said. As if he knew anything about dogs, cats, or trained seals. Mrs. Patterson wouldn't let a stuffed toy into her mausoleum.

"Sit!" Jake repeated.

Oliver sat. Traitor! But his head swung this way and that. Something was off and he knew it. I sniffed and listened. The loamy smell of the wet earth perfumed the air. Nothing more.

Oliver hopped to his feet and trotted away. When he glanced back at me I clicked my tongue and pointed to my heel. He dropped his head and walked back, checking over his shoulder the entire time.

"D'you hear it?" I asked Michael. My voice came out two notes higher than usual.

He squinted and studied the forest. "Yes."

"What?" said Jake, snapping the big wad of gum he'd been chewing since the minute his mom brought him over to our house.

I dug my fingernails into the palms of my hands. "The silence."

Michael shielded his eyes and looked at the muted silver sky.

Jake shrugged. "Yeah, so...?"

"It's never this quiet," I said but tried to sound cool. No need to scare Jake, he was jittery to start with. Then a tree creaked and Oliver started to pant loudly. He raised his hackles and fixed his gaze on some point down the trail. I sucked in another mouthful of clammy air.

"We should go home." Michael sounded uncannily like Tony, the prophet of doom. When I was really little I used to worship Michael. He taught me how to ride a bike and protected me in good ways, like helping me cross the street. Then, when we were both older, he used to babysit me and that's when things went bad. All that power of being in control went to his head. Now, when Tony wasn't around, would-be-king Michael assumed he was the boss. Big mistake.

"C'mon," he ordered and started walking away.

"Not so fast." Let Michael and Jake go home. I could take care of myself, any time, any place. I'd hiked this forest so many times that normally I could hear the trees breathe. I listened again and heard nothing. A prickling sensation of dread ran over me.

I fished a water bottle out of the pocket of my cargo jeans. Jake stopped a few feet in front of me. When he saw I wasn't going anywhere, he smiled at me, as if we were best buds or something. *In his dreams!* I tipped the bottle to my mouth. As I started to drink, the trees shook. I told myself it was just a gust of wind. Then, the ground trembled and a deep rumble rose from below the forest floor. The trembling strengthened to rolling. Water splashed down my face.

A cascade of pine needles fell in thin sheets to the ground. The noise grew louder. A million bass speakers boomed under my feet. Crazy thoughts flashed through my mind: a rock concert, terrorist attack, a bomb. But I knew what it was. An earthquake. We'd had a few small ones this summer, and Tony had been ranting about being prepared.

The ground bucked and kicked. A bear cub ran toward us out of the dark hilly woods. Oliver snarled and leapt at it. The earth pulled sideways and back-and-forth, all at the same time. I dropped to my knees. Rocks and pinecones dug through the denim of my jeans.

"Zeeta!" I screamed. For the first time, the call failed. Oliver feinted around the cub. It rose to its hind feet and glared down at him. Then it dropped to all fours and leaned forward, sniffing curiously. I shrieked *zeeta* over and over. Oliver drew himself up to his grand height of fourteen inches. He deked first to one side of the cub then the other. His mouth worked furiously, warning the cub to stay away. He nipped at its paws. The cub squealed.

"Oliver!" The noise of the quake buried my commands. I crawled toward him, dirt and pine needles sticking to my hands.

Another rolling mound of black fur barrelled down the hill. The mother bear smacked Oliver off the trail with a single swipe. I froze. The ground shifted again and threw the bear on her back. Oliver ran out of the bushes and charged her face. Blood speckled his back leg but he didn't stop attacking. The bear's teeth glinted and snapped. Oliver curled his tail between his legs and flattened his ears. Before I could do anything, he turned and sped away, away from the bears, but worst of all, away from me. The sow lumbered after him, followed by the cub. The thick undergrowth swallowed the three of them. A landslip of rocks poured down the hill and wiped out the place they last stood.

"Zeeta!" The shuddering knocked me flat. "Oliver, come back." The words came out strangled. I didn't know what to do. The roar of the quake drowned everything. My stomach flipped and my mind spun. Earthquake procedures—think!

Jake fell beside me and sweat ran down his face. The park twirled and gyrated in a dance from hell. Trees groaned and crashed to the ground. Branches rained down. Flames of panic burned up my neck. *I'm going to die here. I'm going to die right now!*

I checked over my shoulder for Michael but couldn't see him. A huge ravine had opened on the hill above us. Two colossal evergreens on either side of it lurched and smashed against each other. They held for a split second, and then thundered to the ground. Massive root balls that had clung fast to the soil for hundreds of years were ripped up like anchors. Boulders and rocks plummeted down the slope. The noise pierced my ears.

"Drop and cover!" I screamed at Jake.

He crawled closer to me and curled into a tight ball. I pushed my face into the rough ground. Fine rocks and gnarled twigs bruised and scraped my skin. I dug my face into the dirt. The smell of camping trips and summer filled my head. I loved this smell. *Please let me live to smell it again.* Even though he had been Tony, only Tony, to me for years, ever since he moved out of the house where Michael and I lived with Mom, I cried out, "Daddy."

Think of Oliver, I told myself. When that bear attacked him he looked so scared. He didn't run back to me. He ran away so the bear would chase him and leave me alone. He protected me. Now he was gone.

And here I was, a two-way forward on the Chieftains girls hockey team, whimpering like a baby. Pathetic.

Courage doesn't mean you're not afraid. Tony's mantras surfaced. *It means you hold yourself together in spite of your feelings. S.T.O.P. Stay-Think-Observe-Plan. Above all, stay calm.* I waited for the roiling to stop. *Keep the chimp in the cage. Don't let your emotions take over. Think think think. Listen. Try to figure out what is happening.* I listened. Deep in the park, metal screeching was followed by terrified wailing. The suspension bridge!

CHAPTER 2 | FINDING MICHAEL

NORTH VANCOUVER

Where was Michael? I peered around. Dust kicked up from under the top damp layer of earth. I blinked through the cloud and saw him stagger toward Jake and me. He walked drunkenly as he tried to stay upright on the buckling ground.

Without warning the ravine ruptured past him. It opened and dragged him in. I caught a glimpse of his panic-stricken face and clawing hands. Then he slid out of sight. My throat tightened and the blood rushed out of my head. I gasped for air and called *Michael* but didn't move. Pinecones and small branches littered around me. I covered my head again. *Stay.* I could do that. *Stay calm.* Much harder. What else had Tony drilled into me? *Stay safe yourself. Try to calm others.* In that moment I decided that the quake was not going to beat me. I'd stay strong. I'd stay smart. I'd survive.

Jake was in the tightest fetal position ever. Even though he was older than me, he was totally clueless. I needed to think for both of us. *That's okay I can do that.* I rubbed his arm and he lifted his wild eyes to mine. "Cover your head with your hands!" I shouted and showed him how.

He copied me and a rock rebounded off his laced fingers. His body went rigid. With his face still buried, he gave the okay sign. I covered my head again.

The ground pulled one way, then the other. Rocks tumbled down, pelting our backs, legs, and arms as they rampaged past. The earth was warring with itself and we were its innocent victims. Just as I wondered if it would ever stop and how long I could stay calm, it ended.

A few last boulders paraded wildly down the hill. Flocks of birds burst through the air, chattering indignantly. A great horned owl swooped past. An owl in daytime! One of its feathers floated down to me. Without thinking I caught it and jammed it into my pocket.

I tapped Jake's shoulder and said, "Michael's back this way! We've got to help him."

He looked at me blankly and gulped like a goldfish. At that exact moment he was probably about as smart as one too. Poor guy. It was his first day in the forest. I hoped it wouldn't be his last.

"Michael—we've got to help Michael." I squeezed Jake's hand once and let go before leaping toward the last place I saw my brother. Jake shadowed me. When we got close to the edge of the hole, I dropped to my belly and snaked forward.

Michael dangled, just out of reach, his hands wrapped around a single thin tree root. Terror twisted his face. "Do something—fast! I'm slipping!"

I'd never seen Michael show fear before. Tony didn't allow it.

Behind me the ground bounced with the impact of a falling tree. I locked my teeth together and ordered the shrill voices in my head to shut up.

"Rowan!" Michael's roar slapped away my anxiety.

The ravine yawned broader as I watched. The root ripped out of Michael's hand and he slid farther into the opening wound. He snatched at twigs and tree limbs but the gaping sinkhole sucked him deeper. His eyes stretched wide. His mouth opened in a cry that was lost in the uproar of the scolding birds. I read his lips. "Help!"

Tony said sinkholes could happen anywhere, any time. Especially in earthquakes. *Think. Observe.*

At one end of the hole was a storm water pipe, big enough to stand in. Parts of it had shattered into large pieces. They lay strewn around the sinkhole. Michael fell back and his head thumped against a chunk of broken concrete. A deranged smile flitted across his lips and he closed his eyes. Time slammed to a halt as I gazed at his unmoving body.

"Michael! Michael!"

No response. I was trapped in a nightmare. No one could hear me except Jake, and he was paralyzed with fear. A clinging smell of wet clay and mud rose around me. The ravine hole had gone from ten feet wide to fifteen. How long before Michael was sucked in and swept away? Dirty water dripped from the open pipe and two rats paced anxiously at the opening. I prayed Michael wouldn't see them. Rats drove him crazy.

Behind me, Jake lost his lunch. The smell of partly-digested cheese and root beer gum made me gag.

Stay calm.

"Michael, can you hear me? Say something!"

On the suburban edge of the forest, loud bangs rang out like artillery fire.

Gas explosions and fires come with major earthquakes.

Tony's lessons filled my head. I thought of towering waves dragging helpless victims away from safety. In front of me, murky waters rose around Michael. He stirred and blinked a couple of times.

"I better go home." Jake's words rushed out. Shaking harder than a bobble-head doll, he looked at me with dazed eyes. I kept my tone soft and coaxing, the way I talked to toddlers. "Jake, we can't just go and leave Michael here. He needs help."

Jake moaned. "I can't do anything."

Before I could reply, a loud blast from somewhere close deafened us. Jake's eyes widened. I rubbed his shoulders. "You gotta help us. Please." I gave him my best yearbook smile and nodded encouragement.

A whirlwind of emotions raced through his eyes. At last he nodded.

"Hey!" barked Michael. He pushed himself upright, fully awake now. Bogged by mud, he lifted his feet like an old warhorse. "I gotta get outta here!"

He stomped a single foothold in the clay and rock walls of the gully hole and heaved himself up. The bank crumbled under his feet. As he attempted a second time, the water running into the crevice doubled in volume. Then it tripled. In no time at all Michael was ankle-deep and the water level was rising.

Six inches of moving water can knock a grown man off his feet.

Anyone who'd ever river-fished knew that.

A swell washed the rats into the hole with Michael. They tried to scramble up the steep walls.

Plan.

"Jake! Take off your pants!" I toed off my boots and wriggled out of my jeans. Years of sports had taught me not to be too self-conscious about where I undressed. Still I hated being half-naked in front of Jake. Even when I was fully clothed, he couldn't take his eyes off me. Luckily I was wearing plain black boy-shorts underwear, nothing sexy. I avoided his eyes but I could still feel his creepy teenaged-male hormones radiating toward my body.

"We'll make a rope," I explained to make him think about something else.

Michael braced himself against a boulder. A fresh rush of water surged around him and he saw the rats. His voice jumped an octave. "Hurry!"

Jake stripped to his navy jocks. Then he helped me tie the leg of his chinos to my jeans in a tight reef knot. Michael continued trying to kick steps into the mud wall. Churning brown water swirled up his calves. He leaned into the bank to stay upright.

My pulse pounded in my ears as I watched Jake throw one end of the improvised rope to Michael. "Good," I said to encourage both of us. "Now we're going to anchor this end."

Jake placed his cold hands above and below mine. His touch soothed me in a way I didn't expect. I smiled at him and he smiled back. We could do this. We could save Michael.

"Ready!" Michael sounded half frightened, half angry.

"Go!" I bit my lip. Jake and I lay, shoulders touching, and held tight. The fabric strained and then went taut. Michael grappled his way up the muddy wall. The rope slipped out of his hands. Horror-struck I saw him glide down the slick ridge, into the filthy water. I screamed his name. He fought his way back to the lifeline and grabbed it again. Then he tightened his arms and charged at us. I could hear Tony as if he were beside me. *Show those bastards what you've got. Do it, Morgan!*

"Do it, Morgan!" I roared and tried to sound as ferocious as Tony.

Grunting loudly, Michael hoisted himself up. When he was just an arm's length away, Jake and I extended one hand each and hauled him over the edge. The earth shuddered in an aftershock and Michael lunged past us, took two wobbly strides down the path, and let out a loud whoop. Mud covered every inch of skin and clothing, turning him into a slime monster. He scraped his face and a pale mask opened around his eyes. All about us the forest was rearranging itself. Branches clattered to the ground. An occasional bird squawked. More rocks rolled past us down the hill. A siren lit the air somewhere far away.

We looked at each other in stunned silence. Then we shivered off our fear, fist-bumped, and pretended we hadn't been terrified. I turned away from Jake and dragged on my mucky pants. In the short time since Michael climbed out, the water in the gully had grown to a raging brown torrent. A drenched cat, spinning in the current of the percolating water, was gone before I saw much more than its pointy ears, plastered whiskers and frenzied eyes. Where was Oliver? Guilt pulled at me. In all the confusion and helping Michael, I'd forgotten my best bud. I turned in a circle, hoping to see him. Gone.

"I think we should stay here for a bit. Wait to see if there are any aftershocks or if it's all over for now," I said. "And get Oliver. I don't want to go back without him."

"I think we have to get out of here, Row. That hole's getting bigger by the second and we don't know where it's going to end. Let's get somewhere safe—home."

Michael was losing it. We never called Tony's place home. Since Tony built the place and Mom refused to move in with him six years ago, we'd only lived with him for the summer, like visitors. Working visitors at that.

He bit his lip, wiped more mud from his face, and continued in a whisper. "Look at this." He waved his hand at the damage up and down the thickly forested hill. "This was a major quake. That means there could be some killer aftershocks to come. We *have* to get out of here. Now."

He was right but I didn't want to abandon Oliver. He had saved my life once and I couldn't just leave him there. *Pick your battles.* Mom's voice this time. Where was she anyway? I needed to know, urgently. I checked my phone. *No service.* "Sure," I said, still casting my eyes around for the scouring pad on legs. I called Oliver's name a couple of times but the only answering sounds were birds complaining and water rushing in the gaping gully. He could find his way to Tony's, I told myself. We'd walked here together hundreds of times. He knew the way even though the trail was buried.

The only sure direction was up the hill to the service road that led out of the park. Somehow getting to higher ground seemed like a good idea, especially if any more landslips happened. Michael followed my eyes and nodded but Jake stood fixed to the spot. His hands hung limp at his side. His lips worked silently, as if his vocal chords had been cut.

Another of Tony's Helpful Hints for Natural Disasters popped into my head. *Help calm others.* "Drink?" I offered him my water bottle.

He emptied it in a single slug. "Th...thanks," he stuttered. A moist sheen covered his face.

"Ready?" Michael said as he tightened his bootlaces. Muddy water pressed out of them. "We're going to have to do some bushwhacking." He motioned to the mess above us.

Jake nodded mechanically so I turned and led the charge. Debris and fallen branches tripped us with every step. I thought

I was in good shape but nothing could prepare me for this. I grunted as I wrangled my way from spot to spot. No one said anything and it took about ten minutes to go maybe fifty feet. The sun fought its way out of the clouds and held a spotlight on patches around us. Steam rose from the shaken earth. When I stopped to catch my breath I noticed even super-jock Michael was red-faced and panting.

He looked around, his eyes measuring the destroyed paths and fallen timber. He said, "What we're going to do is...Jake, are you with me here?"

Jake stood motionless. His eyes drifted over the forest and he breathed low and shallow. Perspiration poured down his pasty white face. His pupils were dilated. He looked numb. I hoped he wouldn't faint. If I had to plant my lips on his vomit-coated mouth to revive him, I'd probably puke myself.

"Holy crap, he's in shock," Michael whispered.

I moved to Jake's side. "Hey, Jake, you're going to be fine. C'mon, let's lie down for a few minutes. We could use a rest before we hike any farther." Jake did exactly what I said and I lay down beside him on a mossy patch. "Wow, the clouds are breaking up. I guess that's the end of the rain for today."

As I talked, Michael raised Jake's feet off the ground and propped a large branch under them. I doubted that Jake was really in physical shock but we had to be sure. Tony had forced both Michael and me to take a kajillion first aid courses: baby-sitting first aid, family first aid, summer camp first aid, pet first aid, manic father first aid. I did the courses, aced the exams, and then forgot most of what I learned. But I did remember what to do for shock and so did Michael. We checked Jake from head to foot for any physical injuries. He had a few scrapes on his hands but he wasn't bleeding. He could talk okay. He had psychological shock. Who didn't? His heart was racing and he was close to panic. We had to help him before he got too dazed or depressed.

"Alright, let's practise deep breathing," I said. I touched Jake's stomach. He tightened his abs then relaxed. Helping him helped me; it stopped my urge to get up and run away as fast as I could. "Breathe in and out. Concentrate on making my hand rise and fall with your breaths. Can you do that for me, Jake?"

He nodded and looked at the sky. A creepy stillness settled over the park again. Even the birds stopped their chorus. The quiet calmed Jake and for a while only the sound of our breathing broke the silence.

Then a noise, muffled at first, got louder. The snap and crackle of breaking branches warned that someone or something was moving in our direction. I sat up on one elbow and listened. What now? Michael mouthed the word *bear* and reached for the canister of bear spray on his belt. His hands shook as he yanked it out of the holster.

He motioned to Jake and me to stay put and ducked behind a fallen tree that blocked the north side of the trail. He tiptoed to one end of it and peered through the branches. Then he straightened. Before he said anything I heard faint whistling. *The Gypsy Rover.* My granddad used to whistle that all the time. Sometimes he sang it, raspy and off-key. But here, in the woods, with all this destruction and chaos around us, the casual, cheerful sound froze me to the spot.

NORTH VANCOUVER

"Hello?" I called. "Is someone there?"

"You okay?" A man called back from the other side of the tree. Jake crammed on his boots while I brushed some of the mud off my clothes.

A man swung himself over the fallen tree with the strength and agility of a gymnast. Taller than Michael, which made him well over six feet, he was just as slender. He wore jeans, hiking boots, and a crisp green T-shirt. Dark hair, twisted into dreadlocks, bulged under a bright orange baseball cap. He carried a thick backpack. He scanned us quickly and his eyes locked on Jake.

"Yeah we're cool," Michael said and held his position in front of Jake.

When the stranger spoke, his voice was like dark chocolate, velvety and smooth. He said to Jake, "Hi. I'm Greg Phillips. I'm a paramedic. What's your name?"

A paramedic! He wasn't an axe murderer or a desperate homeless person living in the park illegally. He was someone used to emergency situations. He could even whistle in the face of all this chaos. That made him the best thing that had happened in the last ten minutes.

Jake mumbled his first name only and looked at me, then at Michael, as if he wanted us to tell him what to say next. Michael nudged me and I closed ranks at Jake's side.

Greg kept looking at Jake and I kept staring at Greg even though I knew it was bad manners. A person can go crazy if they focus on the wrong things so I decided to focus on Greg.

"You need a hand, Jake? Anything I can do?" He made it sound as if it would be a privilege to help Jake; it was like he was begging him.

"He's fine," Michael said impatiently. "His breathing's okay, his pulse is fine. He's had a rest and some water. You're okay, aren't you Jake?"

Jake nodded but Greg continued to give him the x-ray vision treatment. Finally he smiled. "Yeah, you seem fine."

He acted as if we'd been waiting for him to come and fix our problems. Maybe he thought only paramedics knew what to do with a freaked-out kid. Michael frowned and I knew that he didn't like the way Greg was trying to take over.

"I've got one thing that might help you." Greg eased off his backpack and rummaged through it. Michael moved closer to me, as if Greg might be going after a weapon or something but Greg pulled out nothing more dangerous than a navy hoodie. He handed it to Jake. "Put this on. You need to keep warm after a shock like that."

In my opinion, Jake didn't need that hoodie. But no one asked me, as usual. Even though it was hot out Jake zipped it up and ran his hands over the front of it. When I recognized the stylized Rod of Asclepius, with a single snake wrapped around it, the universal symbol of healing and medicine, I sighed with relief. Michael raised an eyebrow but I felt better about Greg. I didn't totally trust him yet but at least he probably was who he said he was. And he wasn't trying to get anything from us. He was giving us stuff.

Jake stood a little taller and I had to admit it made him look smarter. He gave his first real smile since the quake. "Thank you."

"You're welcome," Greg said warmly and checked his watch. "We all need to get out of this forest fast. We're damned lucky we're not hurt. But it's taken me this long to hike up from the side of the creek. It's not easy getting around all these slides." He dug in his pack and handed small water bottles to each of us, brand new ones.

Michael checked his to make sure the seal wasn't broken. He narrowed his eyes. "Why're you here? Why aren't you at the bridge, helping people?"

Greg hefted his pack over his shoulder and said low and grave, "The people who were on the bridge are beyond help now."

The few morsels of comfort I'd taken from Greg's appearance shrivelled. I remembered the sound of screams and twisting metal, thought of what must have happened, and pushed the image away. I used to cross that bridge a hundred times a week. The only reason we didn't take it today was because Jake was too scared.

I saw the darkness in Michael's eyes and asked, "Do you think it's the *Big One*?"

Tony's words about The Big One echoed in my brain. *It will change lives, maybe forever. People may die. Thousands maybe. Many more will be hurt.*

Michael shrugged. "Could be."

"We've known for years that the *Big One* was coming," I said. Even as the words left my mouth, I hoped I was wrong.

It was as if Greg was reading my thoughts. "I don't know what a *Big One* would be like, but what I've seen isn't good." He zipped up his pack. "From here on in, kids, it's a matter of keeping your wits about you and surviving. I'm going to hike straight up this hill now. Do you want to follow me or do you have another plan?"

"I wanted to find my dog, Oliver," I said. Michael glowered at me so I added, "But I guess we're going home instead."

I didn't know whether Michael would want to follow this stranger. Jake looked at him too. We all had to agree.

Michael scanned the track before us and behind us. Both were blocked by huge rocks and a few fallen trees. Undergrowth choked the hill above us, the only real escape route. Forget about staying in one place until the aftershocks ended; I wanted to get home. I needed to know that Mom was okay and that Tony had made it back from the gym in one piece. There would be safety in numbers if one of us got hurt. Or if we came across anyone else who needed help. It all depended on Michael. He turned to me and I nodded slightly, just enough to say yes without being eager. I'd have to find Oliver later.

"Why not?" Michael said but it wasn't really a question.

Greg started back up the hill. "I was trying to find my way out of here when I caught a glimpse of purple. By the way I didn't get your names."

Michael smoothed the hem of his purple T-shirt. He spoke first, "I'm Michael. This is my sister, Rowan and our neighbour, Jake."

"Do you live near here?" Greg asked.

"Not far. Over on Parni Place."

I studied the ground so my eyes didn't give anything away. Greg was being friendly and helpful, but Michael lied. Why was he so suspicious?

"Nice to meet you all." Greg did an easy pommel-horse leap back over the fallen tree. Michael struggled to copy him and didn't look as good. I called Oliver a few times while Jake climbed it awkwardly. When I scrambled over, Greg offered his hand to help me down. I hesitated because no one ever thought I needed help doing anything. Being tall and athletic, people treated me as if my height made me invincible or something. I took Greg's warm, strong hand and it felt reassuring. He was just what we needed, someone helpful, someone who had experience in trauma and emergency situations.

I fell in step behind him and he moved at a forced march pace. We clambered over the boulders and pulled our feet through the thick salal bushes that threatened to trip and bury us in the carnage of the forest. Shallow-rooted hemlocks, torn from the ground, sprawled like dead bodies down the hill. Their ghostly limbs quivered in the air.

Michael caught up with Greg and asked, "Where'd you come from?"

"I've been hiking through the woods for a few days. This is beautiful country, or at least it was. When the rain started this morning I hiked out and had lunch at the kiosk. After that I went down to the creek to take pictures." Greg held back a blackberry cane as we filed along the faint path.

Michael rested uphill from him. "Why were you carrying so much water? Isn't that a bit heavy for backpacking?"

"Are you always this curious? I should ask what you were doing in the park."

"We were walking Row's dog. The forest spooks her."

Liar. Michael was talking as if I was a kid again. My anger rose and collapsed before it took flight. This wasn't the time for that battle. Not while the world was in ruins.

"So you weren't just partying?" Greg said.

"Hardly. Rowan and Jake are just kids."

I started to protest but we had reached the park road. At the sight of what lay in front of us, we all fell silent. The surface had mangled and ruptured into five-foot-high peaks that looked like a small asphalt mountain range. A canyon-sized gully had opened along the entire length of the road. Every single tree on that side had fallen over. They blocked access from one side of the road to the other. Root balls leaned on the road, like large dirty bookends.

Michael put his arm around me in a tight, quick hug. He hadn't done that for years and his hold was clumsy and odd. Before he let me go, I felt his heart trying to hammer its way out of his chest. My body went cold, as if I'd been flash-frozen by an ice storm. Jake dropped his water bottle. He opened his hands and spread them like elegant fans at his side. I linked my fingers through his, quickly, and when he squeezed back, I let go. None of us said a word. We just stood and gawked.

Michael checked his cell phone to see if there was service. He shook his head.

"Well, here's another little challenge—but nothing we can't manage, right?" Greg searched Jake's face. Jake smiled at him, even looked him in the eye for a nanosecond.

"Yeah, we'll be okay," Michael said. I knew I would be. I'd survived having Tony as a father. I could survive anything. So what if we faced an obstacle course no matter which way we turned? We could handle it. My next thought was that Tony would be waiting for us, worried. It was never a good idea to worry Tony.

"Excellent," Greg said. "Which way are you headed?"

"That way." Michael jerked his head toward Ross Road.

"Well, I'm parked back there." Greg pointed the other way. "I'd better report to the nearest ambulance depot and see where I'm needed."

"Thanks for the water," I said. Michael started toward home without saying a word.

Jake unzipped the hoodie but Greg put a hand on his shoulder. "Keep it, Jake. Wear it in good health and if our paths every cross again, then I'll be sure to recognize you."

"Thank you," Jake said in the awestruck voice he usually saved for whenever I showed any interest in him.

I chased after Michael who had powered away. "Why were you so rude? You didn't even thank him for the water."

"You're far too trusting," he said and walked a bit faster.

"Why? What didn't you like about him?" I checked over my shoulder to make sure that Greg couldn't hear us. He had disappeared.

"I dunno. It was just weird the way he came out of nowhere, that's all. And his shirt still had the fold lines. No one's clothes look good when they're camping."

"He seemed alright." Jake raced up behind us, rubbing the arms of his hoodie.

"*Oliver*," I called into the broken forest. The sound of sirens screaming a few miles away drowned any hope of hearing him. Useless.

"Come on," Michael said.

Reluctantly I turned to follow him, reassuring myself that Oliver and I had been separated once before in the forest. He found his way home that time. He could do it again. I wanted to get back. Fast.

"So are you going to keep the hoodie?" Michael asked Jake. "What'll your mom say about that?"

"Doesn't matter. It's mine. I've thought about becoming a paramedic." Jake spoke, barely opening his mouth. Paramedic? Two seconds ago he needed rescuing himself.

We climbed a hill of fallen trees and picked our way around the yawning cracks in the road. At last we walked out of the park and my heart somersaulted. The street looked like it had been bombed. Huge canyons had been ripped through it. The nose of a car poked out of one of the crevices. Two telephone poles were down and the rest leaned at crazy angles. One of the power lines was severed. A live wire whipped and snapped in violent patterns, crackling noisily over the sidewalk and street. Michael, Jake and I crossed to the other side of the road. People gathered in their front yards. People I had never seen in the neighbourhood before milled about, squinting as if they were half blinded. In front of a pseudo-Tudor house a swarthy man in a black T-shirt and board shorts punched numbers into his cell phone as if the force of his actions could restore service. Behind him, a woman sat on the front steps and crooned mournfully to her baby. Shattered glass covered the lawn.

Where was Mom? Was she okay?

Don't think about that now. *Focus on the situation at hand. When the immediate situation is secured and safe, see who else you can assist.* So many people right there in front of us. I wondered if we should ask if anyone needed first aid but what could we offer without even a Band-Aid between us? Breathing in the smoke and dust, I listened to the anxious voices. Helplessness rushed over me.

"Rowan." Michael touched my shoulder and I followed him. A million feelings pulled me a million directions but I refused to crumble.

Then the earth shifted.

"Drop and cover," I barked, strong and authoritative—not an ounce of panic in my voice. I was a great actor.

The dark-shirted man hit the ground. The woman curved her body over her baby's. Michael, Jake, and I dived for the sidewalk and covered our heads. I couldn't stop myself from peeking out from the crook of my arm. The house in front of me shimmied in a violent voodoo jig. The last of the glass in the front windows splattered across the lawn. I covered my ears and hoped it wasn't another big one. How long would it go on?

An explosion on the other side of the street made me lift my head again. The house by the live power line burst into flames. In front of me the woman with the baby wailed loudly. The man crawled over to her side. Somewhere a dog howled. Oliver? No. The tone was too deep. People screamed. Goosebumps ripped up and down my arms.

When the tremor ended, the sidewalk had a six-foot trench in the middle of it.

Jake took one look and erupted in loud, nervous laughter. He sat and hugged his knees to his chest. Then he threw back his head and laughed louder.

Suddenly I was laughing too. People might be dying I reminded myself. Why am I laughing? But I couldn't stop. Jake and I laughed until we were breathless and tears ran down our faces.

Michael lay flat on his back with his eyes closed. He had bitten his bottom lip and blood dripped down his chin.

CHAPTER 4 | VANCOUVER
—FIRST WAVE

VANCOUVER, WEST END

Dixie Morgan locked her bike to the rack and went into the Belleville Café. She ordered a skinny latte, in spite of the humid heat and the sweat pouring down the middle of her back. She carried the steaming mug to a table beside the window. Over by the espresso machine her cycling partner, Ben, flirted with the blond barista. The barista smiled and made him a double shot at no extra charge. Dixie ripped open an envelope of artificial sweetener and dumped it into her coffee. At first she thought the vibrations came from the roadwork outside. Then the glass bottles behind the bar started jumping off the shelves.

Dixie sat, riveted to the spot, arrested by disbelief. What was it Tony said to do in an earthquake? She had been too busy laughing at his paranoia about the *Big One* to listen. The kids told her that he wasn't wrong. It wasn't a question of *if*, but *when*. She always answered that he was selling fear and she wasn't buying.

Only when the scalding coffee splashed against her hands did she snap out of her daze. The plate glass window vibrated. She shoved the mug across the table and launched herself out of her seat. As the force of the tremor flung her against the sharp edge of a table, breaking glass showered down on the spot where she had been sitting. She fell to her knees and her head hit the floor. Tables and chairs cantered around her. The barista was nowhere in sight. Ben sheltered under a wooden table, holding onto a leg of it. *The walls are strongest in the washroom. I'm sure that's what Tony said.* She clawed past the spinning, bouncing furniture. Deafened by the sound of the world exploding, Dixie rounded a corner to the back rooms. At that exact moment the under-engineered walls of the building started to buckle. A cloud of concrete dust blinded and choked her and she patted the ground, trying to find safety. No such place existed and she swayed on the edge of oblivion. As the arch over the hallway collapsed, her homing thoughts flew to her children. *Mikey! Rowan! Listen to your father!*

VANCOUVER, DOWNTOWN

The hotel receptionist pulled up Linda's account on the computer with inch long, multi-coloured fingernails. Linda Patterson wondered idly how the girl—because she couldn't be a day over sixteen—was able to type. When the receptionist handed over the swipe machine, the phone rang and the girl pushed her gum into her cheek to answer it. Linda tapped in the PIN for her Visa. $2,000 for one night. A deluxe suite, spa treatments, room service breakfast and dinner for everybody. It was all worth it to see her sister Wendy happy after decades of being a bridesmaid. Linda had wanted it to be the best bachelorette party ever, and it was.

Transaction approved. Please remove card. Linda slipped her card out of the machine and into her wallet. The paintings on the wall behind the reception desk started to sway. The receptionist looked up at her from under peacock-blue eyelids and her mouth made a small "o." As the quake gained momentum, the man waiting to check out next grabbed Linda's wrist and dragged her into the lobby.

"Get down—under a chair," he said. Linda slid across the marble floor on her belly and pushed her head and shoulders under a leather wing chair. She held on to its scuffed legs and thought about her son, Jacob. She knew he was in Tony Morgan's house and probably a lot safer than she was. Above the screech of the bending building she heard a shrill scream. Horrified, she realized the voice was hers.

CHAPTER 5 | BE IT EVER SO HUMBLE

NORTH VANCOUVER

We jogged after that, as if we could outrun any more after-shocks. On our street, only one house was seriously damaged. It was the old two-storey place that used to belong to my grandparents. The front wall looked as if it had been smashed by a wrecker's ball. Bricks lay scattered across the lawn like busted teeth. The Kurtz family who owned it now were away for a week. I was getting paid to feed their cat. Where was Misty now?

The image of animals caught in the muddy water of the devil's gully flickered in my mind. I shook my head to erase the memory.

And where was Oliver?

Oliver's okay, I told myself. I decided to believe that until I knew otherwise.

One neighbour's house had a collapsed porch and side deck. The roof of another sagged. Perhaps that's how they always were, I couldn't remember. All the front windows were shattered. People clustered outside. They didn't lift their eyes as we walked past. It was as if the earthquake had turned everyone into zombies. Their zoned-out faces filled me with dread. I knew Tony had a doomsday cache of food and water but how many people could we help?

The only neighbour by himself was Mr. Kagome who was about a thousand years old. He sat on the lawn in lotus position and gazed at his drooping porch. He was an odd bod at the best of times. He did stuff like Tai Chi and old man yoga. I figured he was a Buddhist or something, which had to be why he was so peaceful now. He watched his house in complete silence, as if waiting to see what it might do next. All he wore was blue boxer shorts and a large gold crucifix. I guess he was too old to be shocked.

Tony's house at the end of the cul-de-sac stood straight and tall, just like he said it would after an earthquake. The thought of my basement bedroom, cool and safe and miles away from all this insanity, drew me like a magnet. Inside the tall chain-link fence that surrounded the place, stood Tony's truck. As we got closer, I saw him hunched over at the far end of the yard. I whooped and ran faster. Toward him, toward safety and sanctuary. Tony stood and saluted. He wore thick gardening gloves. I smiled but he didn't smile back.

When I was a kid, we used to be really close and every time I came to see him, he'd greet me with a huge smile. We used to do fun stuff together: camping, hikes, Playland in summer. But the older I got, the more he seemed to disapprove of everything I did. He didn't like the way I walked, the way I talked, the way I breathed. Then the motorcycle argument blew away the last traces of his approval.

In three months and two weeks I'd get my driver's licence. I had my eye on a lime green Kawasaki Ninja and had saved almost enough to buy one. After all, I rode trail bikes almost as soon as I could walk. Even tearing down rough hills and pushing through the thick mud I stayed upright. Nothing was finer than the feeling of flying over the earth, inhaling a lungful of fresh air. A road bike was the next, natural progression. Then I'd go on long, long rides out to the country and leave behind everything that made me sad or angry. I'd be free.

Mom understood that I had to be two things: who and what I wanted. I thought Tony would be happy too. Before he and Mom split up, the whole family used to go on long bike rides together. Mom and I still biked together on spring break. I thought he understood this part of me but when I told him I'd found a Ninja for sale near his house, he went ballistic.

"Motorbikes are dangerous."

"You'll get wet when it rains."

"Girls on bikes look butch."

"You're too young."

"You have no idea how expensive it's going to be."

I argued that he was the one who taught me how to ride a dirt bike and he should trust me on one that was street legal. He said he trusted me but he didn't trust all the other drivers out there. I said I would be careful. He said no one could be that careful. Every time it ended with me storming down to my bedroom and slamming the door. The more he talked, the more I wanted one. And I was going to get one too. Then I'd never tell him where I was going.

I'd never know what I could do if I didn't try different things. Tony wanted me to be like him, to do the things he'd done growing up. He wanted to stand over me and make all my choices and decisions. I could think for myself but he refused to let me.

As if my future bike was his business anyway. I lived with Mom for most of the year and she said as long as I did the road safety course and proved I could handle a bike responsibly, I could have one. So Tony would have to accept it. If he didn't, that was his problem.

Ever since that fight he'd been frowning at me. First he didn't like my lipstick. Then he said I was reading garbage and ruining my brain. Last week he said I wasn't getting enough exercise and wouldn't make the hockey team in the fall. What he couldn't see was that I didn't need him to organize my life. But that didn't stop him from trying. I don't know what happened to my father—the man who taught me how to skate, change a bicycle tire, and make the best mushroom risotto in the world—but I wished someone would send him back and take away this grouch.

With all that'd happened I hoped maybe now he'd be happy to see me. What did I get instead? A thunder face glowering at me from the inside of the security fence. Situation normal.

"Where've you kids been? I've biked around the neighbourhood in a methodical grid about a dozen times searching for you." The smell of Tony's garlic and onion breath travelled the six feet between us. "Well, it looks like you haven't suffered any major injuries. Good. That would be a complication we don't need."

"Yeah, we're here and ready to serve," Michael said casually in the way Tony, with his RCMP background and love of formal protocol, called sarcastic and disrespectful. Michael knew he was safe from Tony's wrath because he'd aced all his final exams again, and in two weeks would be packing to go back to university on a full scholarship. Tony had been boasting to everyone about how smart Michael was. That gave Michael a get-out-of-jail free card for all minor offences, and I became the focus of all Tony's frustration.

Tony switched off the radio in his shirt pocket and unlocked the front gate. The new padlock that shone in the sun hadn't been there when we went out earlier. He motioned Michael and me into the yard, but put his arm out to stop Jake. "Sorry. Family only," he said with the warmth of an iceberg.

"God, Tony," I said and edged a little closer to Jake to show him I was in his corner. "He has to stay with us until his mom gets home."

Jake let his long black hair swing across his face like he was trying to hide. His house was right behind ours, on another cul-de-sac, connected by a pedestrian path.

Although our homes were physically close, the people who lived in them inhabited different universes. But wasn't an earthquake the time for intergalactic cooperation?

Tony held his flinty eyes on mine. "This is an emergency situation. It isn't a time to be sentimental. When essential services are operating, even at emergency levels, then we might shelter others. We might even share some of our supplies. Until that happens we close ranks and take care of our own. Family is the only thing that matters at this point."

He said all that really fast like he'd practised it several times. He believed his opinions were facts, laws even. I searched for a comeback that wouldn't trigger his temper but I couldn't find one. His jaw flexed, a warning sign that he was about to blow his top.

Angry words leapt to my mouth but I swallowed them. I needed time to make a different plan to rescue Jake. So I walked away. "Fine. Whatever." My insides curdled; Jake wasn't exactly disaster savvy, and who knew where his mom was.

When she asked Michael and me yesterday if we'd like to go for dinner and a movie with Jake, and then could he stay overnight, both of us said yes. We didn't tell Tony that we had been bribed into inviting Jake over. If we told him now...well it just wasn't worth the grief. When Tony made a rule, he never, ever changed his mind.

Still, couldn't he see that Jake and his mom were alone? He had lots of space in his house and Jake's dad was overseas working. Okay, so maybe he didn't want to invite both of them to stay. Still he could put Jake up for a couple of hours, at least until his mom came home. Tony had a heart of stone.

I was halfway to the front steps when his voice hit me like a fist. "Rowan!"

"What?" I spun around. To my surprise, Jake was marching away, head high, like a soldier on dress parade.

"Where's the canine?" Tony said.

"Oliver?" That's all he was to Tony, the dog, the canine, the fleabag. My anger folded into despair. "Isn't he here? He ran away in the forest. I'd hoped..." I looked around the yard as if he might magically materialize.

I choked on the thought of loyal, brave Oliver alone in that messed-up forest. When I got him from the shelter I'd promised him no one would ever hurt him again. I promised him he'd never be hungry again. I tried to tell myself that he was well trained, that he had been coming to Tony's house for every summer since I got him. It didn't help.

Panic jolted me and I knew I had to find him. Now. We'd reported in. Tony knew we were safe. There was no reason for me to stick around. I strode toward the gate but Tony snapped the lock shut.

"No one goes anywhere without my permission. And I'm not giving my permission for the next twenty-four hours at least. I've been listening to the radio reports. This wasn't just a big one it was the *real* big one. Magnitude 9.5."

9.5. I gasped. Tony loved big earthquake stories but I couldn't remember one that big before. The hair on my neck bristled. I felt disconnected from everything around me. It was as if I was watching the scene from a different dimension. Michael said something low and ferocious under his breath.

"To make matters worse, it was a shallow one. It hit from here to Oregon and beyond. The epicentre was close, just off Vancouver Island; a tsunami alert has been issued. It's insane out there and it's going to be chaos for a while."

His face glowed, as if the quake was everything he had hoped it would be and more. He was ready, readier than most people might guess. From where we stood I could hear the generator humming in the back yard. I thought about the house and its spare bedroom, the storage cellar, and the water tanks. He could look after a hundred Jakes if he wanted to. Instead he was turning his back on the world.

"Don't worry, we're well provisioned to ride it out, but we're just not going to share. Not yet." He handed Michael a key on a lanyard. "You and I will be the gatekeepers. This key opens the padlocks on this gate and the one on the driveway"

"Where's *my* key?" I asked.

"Sorry," Tony said. "You have to be sixteen or older to have a key to this gate."

I should chain myself to the fence. A dozen more fast replies sprang to my mind. *Pick your battles.* "I'll go phone Mom."

"How're you going to do that?" Tony's face softened and he spoke kindly. Kindly wasn't good. He reserved kindness for only the most extreme situations and a shiver of panic ran over me. He didn't notice, just kept listing the horrors we couldn't see. "Power's out and phone lines are down over the entire city. Cell towers are down too. The cable network's cut.

You've got to trust that your mom'll phone or email her parents in Calgary when she can, just like we will. That's the protocol for emergency situations."

Then he hugged me, the same way Michael did at the park. It felt just as odd, only Tony's heart wasn't racing the way Michael's had. For a minute I was eight years old again, trying not to cry after being benched for a month because I refused to wear my hockey helmet. Back then Tony's strong arms and gentle words made me feel better. But that magic was gone. I thought about how he'd turned Jake away and wrestled free of him.

He made a big show of pulling out his truck keys. "A few houses like ours will have their own generators but most people won't have phone or power. It'll be a while before things are normalized again."

Normalized again. He always talked like a dictionary or a newsreader. Couldn't he just say *back to normal* like a regular person? I resumed my fight stance.

Tony didn't notice. "Now that you're back, I'm going out to check what's left in the stores before they're sold out. Or looted. But first I'll stop by Javi's place and make sure they're okay."

"So you get to see everything but we don't?" I followed him to the truck. I wanted to know the real reason he was going out. We had enough food for everyone on the entire North Shore.

Tony's instant anger would have turned some kids to stone but I didn't blink. His voice was low and cold. "I'm not going out for a sick look at other people's problems. I'm going to do recon, see how bad the roads are, how widespread the damage is. I'm going to evaluate the situation overall. People are being told to stay put. That means you. You're safe as you can be behind these gates. Neither of you are to go in or out of this yard. Do not share supplies with anyone. Family first, family only. No one else. Do you understand?" He frowned.

Michael nodded, his face stony. I copied him.

"So lock the gate behind me, Michael. And both of you— remember the rules."

Michael picked up the lock and, with a big flourish and a smirk at me, used his key to open it. That didn't take long. Two seconds after the biggest earthquake ever and Michael was already sucking up to Tony again. I didn't need some ancient philosopher to tell me that power corrupts. I tried to ignore him, but I wanted a key of my own and I couldn't help glaring at him. Great. My hostility sunk me down to his level. Michael and I were like leopards, we couldn't change our spots.

Meanwhile, Tony's jaw flexed again. He climbed into the truck, pinning me with his eyes. I made a few fast decisions of my own and answered quietly, "Okay."

"Right." Tony gave me one last, sharp look. It was as if he was reading my mind so I tilted my head and tried to appear innocent. He started the truck and said, "While I'm gone both of you grab a shower. Rowan, do some laundry and get the mud out of those clothes. Michael, you get that roll of wire laid out. When I get back we'll string it along the top of the fence."

I stole a glance to where I'd last seen Jake. He had only faked going home and hovered on the greenway path next to our fence. He seemed to be eavesdropping. Tony hadn't noticed him so I looked away quickly.

Tony rolled down his window. "Rowan, I'll be back soon. You'd better get busy."

I'll get busy don't you worry about that. I threw him the eye bite. He slapped the outside of the truck's door, wheeled around and drove off. When he was out of sight, Jake started to walk away. He headed toward his house as if he might find his mother there. For his sake I hoped he did.

CHAPTER 6 | HELPING FRIENDS

NORTH VANCOUVER

Michael closed the driveway gate. I tapped my toe, reviewing my plans. First on the list: Jake. Even if Tony couldn't see it, Jake needed us. Me. He needed someone. This was a terrible time to be alone.

Michael poked me in the ribs. "Shouldn't you get moving?"

I pushed his hand away. "When I'm good and ready. I've got more important things to do right now."

He pointed to the bale in the corner of the yard. "Do you see what I have to do? That's razor wire in case you didn't notice."

"Razor wire? Get out of here."

"It's just the start of Tony's master plan. He's going to keep out the world."

"Whoa. Has he totally lost it or what?"

"This is the best thing that's ever happened to him. You know he's been preparing for this ever since Nana and Pop died. Now he can tell the world he got it right and everyone else got it wrong."

"Harsh." But he was right. Ever since our grandparents—Tony's parents—were killed in an earthquake in Japan years ago, Tony had been even spookier about quakes than he was before. He used the money they left him to build a seismically reinforced house.

House? It was a survivalist's dream surrounded by raised garden beds. Tony said that when the Big One hit people would need to have their own food supply. So he grew vegetables and kept chickens. Whenever Michael and I visited, we became slaves to his garden, his brood of brown, black and grey hens, and his lunacy. Only now Tony seemed like the smartest guy on the block.

Buried under the garden beds were two 25,000-litre tanks, one of water and one of propane. The propane would power the generator and the barbecue with enough left over to heat the basement for up to six months. Tony could keep us locked inside that fence forever.

I couldn't help those people around the corner whose houses were burning. I couldn't go back to the forest and find Oliver. But I was going to do something to help somebody and that somebody was Jake. He'd been wrapped in cotton wool his entire life. He probably couldn't open a can of beans if they had one in their organic-vegan, fun-starved house.

"Give me your key," I said.

Michael's hand flew to the end of the lanyard. "Why?"

"I'm not leaving Jake all alone until his mom gets home. *If* she gets home. I'm bringing him back here."

"And what're you going to do with him then?"

"He can stay in your room until his mom gets back."

"Tony'll go ballistic if he finds him."

"Yeah, so? Then it'll be too late. If he finds out, he'll have to let Jake stay. Or he'll have to push him out of the gate and if you and I refuse to help, that'll be pretty hard to do."

"What if his mom doesn't get back today? What if he has to stay overnight again?"

"Then that's twice the reason to help him, isn't it?"

"Tony said no."

"C'mon. You know what Jake is like. He can barely get milk out of a carton. When we took Mrs. Patterson's money for the movie and dinner, we were kind of giving her our word to look after Jake. We *have* to help him." I didn't point out that Michael was the one who took the money, chose the restaurant, and the movie. Michael pocketed the change, not me.

Michael shook his head.

I reached for the lanyard. "Give."

"No." Michael stepped away.

"Give me that key now...or..." I put my hands on my hips. He squinted. "Or what?"

I bit my lip. I'd been hanging on to my trump card for so long, I almost hated to play it. *One favour earned for every secret learned.*

"Pirates' Code. I was using your laptop the other day..."

"You bitch."

I thought of backing down but I didn't. There would be one right thing in this sea of wrong today, even if I had to fight dirty to get it. "Honestly, Michael, I don't care if you're two-spirited, GBL *or* T. Who does? But you and your boyfriend shouldn't be making videos of yourselves. What are you going to do with them, anyway? Post them on YouTube? Tony's not as open-minded as Mom is and if he knew you were singing love songs to each other you'd never hear the end of it. If he knew you guys were doing a little weed at the same time, who knows? He might even turn you in to his cop buddies."

Michael had come out, but Tony didn't want to believe him. He said Michael hadn't even had a serious girlfriend yet so how could he be sure? Michael's usual answer was that Tony hadn't had a boyfriend yet so how did he know he didn't like guys better? Then they'd yell at each other until one of them stomped out of the room. Tony might argue with Michael about his sexual orientation, but drugs were another matter. Being a retired cop, a former Mountie in this exact neighbourhood, Tony had a zero tolerance policy when it came to illegal substances.

Michael fingered the key. "Sometimes I hate you."

"Join the club," I said with a slight twinge of guilt. "Sorry but I need to do something to help someone right now—and Jake needs help as much as anyone."

Michael gave me a sidelong glance and sighed. Even with traces of blood on his mouth, he was rugged handsome. Life was easy for a smart jock like him. Easy in all ways but one, the hardest one.

"But you're going to help me, aren't you?"

Michael rubbed his chin with the back of his hand. "I'm not giving you the key though. I'll let you out the gate. I'll be here when you get back. Hey, wait a sec." He rifled through Tony's tool bag and found the gas shut-off wrench. "Take this."

These wrenches were given to anyone who took the base level emergency preparedness course, which meant probably two houses in our entire neighbourhood might have one. We did, and for now that was all that mattered. And we didn't have to ask Tony if he'd shut the gas off. He could teach those courses if he wanted to.

"Be careful," Michael said and waved me through the gate. I swung the tool like a cudgel and walked between the two tall fences that bordered the public path. If I kept moving, I could keep the soul-shakes away. Mom's voice found me again. *Soul-shakes wrap you in a blanket of negative energy. Negative energy steals your strength. Take that blanket of worry and negativity and pack it away in a box. Then you can stop worrying about things you can't change.* She would lead me in a charade of folding a big, heavy blanket and stuffing it into an imaginary box. Then she'd put her arm around me and envelope me with the light scent of her Lady Millions cologne. Icy fingers crept up my spine. *Where was Mom?* My biggest fears grabbed me again. My other fears—running out of food, caring for Jake if his mother didn't come home—we could manage somehow. But where was Mom? I couldn't handle not knowing that. I wanted her here with us, in the safest house in the world.

But Mom said she would never live with Tony again. When he built this place with his inheritance, he said she'd like it once it was finished. Instead they had huge fights over what she called his disaster paranoia. She refused to spend even a single night in it, so he moved in without her and without Michael and me.

Mom liked being close to the beach, to downtown, to all the members of her pack. But what if our house in Kitsilano was wrecked? Would Tony let her live here now? I stopped myself mid-thought. *Can't fix it. Don't touch it.* I imagined picking up the huge dark blanket of worry and folding it as small as a facecloth, determined to be strong. Absorbed in my mental steps of folding, packing and closing, I turned into Jake's yard and whistled through my teeth.

His house was on its knees. The front steps had shifted forward and caved in. The roof was broken like a letter V, as if had been struck with a massive axe. The columns that supported the covered porch tilted toward the street at a dangerous angle. Jake sat on the wall of the front drive with a guitar case at his feet and a backpack on his lap. His arms were folded over his pack and his head rested on them. The stench of rotten eggs curled around my nostrils.

"Jake." I ran to him. "We've got to turn the gas off and go back to my place."

Jake sat up so abruptly he almost fell over. "Your dad said I couldn't stay."

"Screw him. But we've got to turn off the gas first."

"Don't know how." He rolled his eyes like a skittish horse.

"C'mon, time to learn some basic coping skills." I tried to sound friendly, but Jake leaned away from me. I took his pack and grasped his hand. His skin felt as clammy as raw chicken. "Do you want to be one of these helpless people who dies waiting for someone else to come along and save them? Don't you want to be independent someday?"

He hesitated so I dragged him to the side of the house.

"That's your gas meter." I pointed to it. "The wrench goes over the valve here and then you turn it a quarter turn so it's crosswise to the pipe." I put his hand on the wrench and guided it through the turn. "Easy peasey, huh? Now your house won't burst into flames at a single spark."

Jake was staring past me. There, standing on the street, was the stranger from the forest, Greg. He waved. I waved a little too enthusiastically, happy to see someone who might help me with Jake. Greg looked different in the bright sunshine, away from the shadows of the forest. Silver hairs showed in his dreadlocks and he seemed older than just an hour ago. He had prominent canine teeth and his smile was wolfish. Still, his positive energy and confidence touched me like a soothing breeze.

"Weren't you going to help at the hospital?" I asked, sounding nosy like Michael.

"Some people up here needed help." He flicked his head down the block. "Minor cuts and contusions only. Then I saw a jacket I recognized. It's Jake, right? Is this your house?"

I moved between Jake and Greg. "I'm just about to take him to my place. Our house is okay."

Greg's dark eyes sparkled. "Good. I'm glad that Jake's got a safe place to go. Excellent work on the gas meter, Jake. If I were you, I'd stay with this woman. She knows what to do."

At the word *woman* I smiled, even though I felt kind of manipulated by it. He was flattering me to make me trust him and it worked for one shiny second. It also seemed to calm Jake who grinned and rocked on his heels.

Greg waved and left and I wondered what he had really been doing in that forest. Finding us once was coincidence. Finding us twice seemed strange. What would Tony say if he saw me talking to him? I tried not to think about Tony's bitter philosophy: *when the world gets turned upside down, the bottom feeders end up on top.* If Jesus Christ, the Prophet Muhammad, and Buddha were rolled into one person and came back to save us, Tony would slam the door in his face. Paramedic or not, Greg wouldn't get Tony's stamp of approval even if I thought he had essential skills.

I tapped my toe. "Okay we're done. Let's get outta here. We're going back to my place."

"But your dad—"

"—doesn't have to know." Nervousness burned a hole in my stomach as the seconds ticked away. "Michael and I've got a plan."

"I dunno. Need to phone my mom." He sank down and sat cross-legged. "Our phone's not working."

"No one's phone is working." God. Should it be this hard to help someone? "C'mon Jake, you can stay in Michael's room again and Tony won't even know you're there."

"What if Mom comes home?" He lay back and rested a hand on the guitar case.

"She knows you were with us, right? No big mystery." I tried to direct his attention to something else. "You risked your life to get a guitar out of a wrecked house?"

"It was my dad's."

"Your dad plays guitar?" I tried to imagine Mr. Patterson, with his bald head dotted with brown spots, bent over a guitar. I couldn't imagine him singing. He had a voice like a wet cat.

"No. My dad's dead." Jake hugged the guitar case to his chest.

"God, no! I'm so sorry. I didn't know. Your mom said he's working in Turkey."

"Not *him*," he said quietly. "My real dad."

"Real dad?"

"He died before I was born. Mom said he liked country music. He bought this guitar with his first paycheque. Mom kept it for me."

By Jake's standards that was a speech and the effort seemed to wear him out. His hair fell in a curtain in front of his face.

"All the more reason for you to come to my place. You know that Michael has a huge bedroom. There's lots of space for you and your guitar." *Please hurry. Tony could be back any minute.*

Jake didn't move for the longest time and I didn't say a word. If he was anything like the guys in my family I knew the more I argued, the more he would resist. I tried not to hyperventilate thinking about the explosion if Tony got home and I wasn't there. Just when I was ready to abandon Jake, the earth rippled below us. Glass shattered in nearby houses. Some people cried out. It ended almost before it began.

Jake's head jerked up and he scrambled to his feet. "Okay, I'm coming."

"Good. But don't breathe a word about Greg showing up."

Jake nodded dumbly and I didn't explain any more than that. I didn't say that Tony and Michael saw stranger-danger everywhere, as if I was some sort of first-grader. I turned and power-walked in the direction of Tony's place. I let Jake pass and go in front. I wanted to make sure he didn't faint before we got there.

His head swivelled back and forth as he checked around him. He threw his feet out in front of him like he expected his hiking boots to start doing the walking for him. Actually Michael's old boots, because Jake didn't own any. Mrs. Patterson told Michael that the forest was a place where terrorists and pedophiles hung out and Jake was forbidden to go there. I guessed that's why Michael brought Jake to the forest today; he felt sorry for him. Jake never talked about friends, only about things he did with his parents, mostly his mother.

That's why she asked Michael and me to be rent-a-pals for the night. She said she was worried that Jake was spending too much time alone. Michael was too nice to say no, or maybe he just wanted the night out because, like me, he was saving every dime.

Jake and Mrs. Patterson were like no other people I'd ever met. She trusted Jake in Tony's house because Tony was a retired cop, which shows what she knew about people. Tony took care of Tony first, then Michael, and last of all me. Jake wasn't even on the list. As head of the Neighbourhood Watch

Mrs. Patterson thought she knew everybody and their business but she only knew their outsides.

When Jake and I reached the end of the pedestrian path, Tony's truck was sitting outside our house. I grabbed Jake's shirt and hauled him back behind the hedge. I crouched and put my finger to my lips. Jake stared at me with fresh terror in his face. I was babysitting a sixteen-year-old. And I wasn't getting paid for it.

CHAPTER 7 | ROOMMATES

NORTH VANCOUVER

Life had shifted sideways, like the torn asphalt at my feet.

Tony's voice stabbed through the air. "Tell Rowan I expect *all* the laundry to be done by the time I'm back, not just her clothes."

"Will do," Michael yelled over the roar of the pickup. The taillights disappeared down the street and I exhaled for the first time in a century. I signalled all clear to Jake and charged to the front gate.

"Where the hell've you been?" Michael snapped the lock open.

"Jake wasn't sure if he wanted rescuing or not," I said. "What was Tony doing back?"

"There's a deer with a broken leg in Javier's yard."

"Tony's best friend and hunting buddy," I said to Jake. "And?"

"He came to get a rifle to put it out of its misery. And his field-dressing kit." I thought about Tony's nylon carry case with the axe, knives, saws, and gut hook for turning a dead deer into venison. He'd be gone for hours. "Did he notice I wasn't here?"

"Yeah right. He didn't even get out of his truck—made me get everything while he waited."

"Typical." I wiped my sweaty palms on my jeans. "Anyway Jake's place is totalled. Good thing the sheets are still on the trundle bed in the TV room. We'll just move it into your room and we'll be ready for a party. I'll see if I can find some noise-makers and loot bags." I joked to try to calm Jake. Only I really didn't know how to do that. Nothing in all my emergency and first aid training taught me how to look after nervous people. We'd all been through minor shakes this summer but still Jake seemed unprepared on so many levels. Like a lot of people he probably figured we'd never have a big one.

He peered past me. "How come your place is still okay?"

"It's new technology—Tony built it to protect us against earthquakes. Crazy, right? I mean, to be protected we actually had to be in the house at the time of the quake. But there'll be aftershocks probably for a few days yet and it'll keep us safe through all of those. Time to get you settled downstairs, okay?"

When Jake only nodded slightly, I kept talking. "You see that old brick house at the end of the street? That was our grandparents' place when they were alive. You don't see many brick houses in Vancouver, do you? The grands owned all this land and then Tony inherited all of it. He sold off everything but the three lots where his house is. He chose the sunniest spot." I paused and tried to stop myself from babbling on even more. In a single burst I had broken one of Tony's rules about fifteen different ways: keep family business private.

Michael came to my rescue. "What Rowan's trying to tell you is that Tony's place is engineered to extreme seismic standards."

Jake studied his shoes and coughed. "When can I phone my mom?"

"Could be days before anyone has phone service," Michael said. "Cell towers are down. Landlines are out."

At that news something in Jake cracked. His body shrank as if all the blood had been sucked out of it.

Michael punched Jake lightly on the shoulder and offered his usual solution to any crisis. "C'mon you guys, I'm hungry. I'm going to crack into the emergency chips and chocolate."

Jake followed us up the steps to the wide, reinforced front porch that wrapped around the house. It was a rampart and Tony patrolled the immediate area from it. There were no trees or bushes near the building, nothing that anyone could hide behind. Garden beds crammed the yard. On the other side of the back fence, in Jake's back yard, there was a tall cedar hedge that blocked our view of his house fifty feet away. Raspberry canes lined our side of that fence, making a prickly moat. Four mature fruit trees, two apple, one pear, one plum, had been preserved at the far corners of the property lines.

I took Tony's wooden rocking chair. Jake pulled the green plastic loveseat next to me and flopped into it. If he got any closer, he'd be sitting in my lap. I inched away from him and the creak of the rocker filled the silence. Smoke from a dozen different fires streaked the sky, like our old lives drifting away.

When Michael came back from the kitchen he had two cold cut sandwiches with mayonnaise and mustard oozing out of the sides. He handed Jake his special request, a cheese one. Then he passed out water bottles, bags of potato chips, and chocolate bars.

"Eat slowly. We'll be on rations for a while," he said and bit his sandwich in half.

He raised his small binoculars and scoped out the street. The people who lived at the corner were hefting one large box after another out of their truck. Tony told us after an earthquake there would be looting. Seeing his prophecy come true made my first mouthful of sandwich sink like lead in my gut.

"Harsh," Michael said. "Let's see—someone's got a flat screen TV, like it's going to do them any good with no power." He shook his head. "Doesn't take long, does it? The quake was barely two hours ago and people are cleaning out the stores."

As he spoke, the earth shook. The house rode the shock absorbers of its reinforced steel foundation. Inside a few books hit the floor. Anything that could be nailed down in the house was. The only loose objects were unbreakable.

The tremor stopped and I slowly peeled back the wrapper of my chocolate bar, putting on a show of coolness for Jake. I let a piece melt slowly under my tongue.

Michael flipped his unopened bar in the air. "While you were at Jake's, I listened to the radio. There're fires all over the place, waterlines are in pieces, lots of injuries. I'm guessing probably some deaths too. It's chaos. No one can get from Vancouver to the North Shore yet because both bridges have been closed."

"They were supposed to be safe," Jake protested as if his words could change the facts. I wished they could.

"They were ready for deep quakes but it seems no one expected one this shallow or this close. There're police barricades on both ends of both bridges." Michael shifted in his seat.

Jake gulped his chocolate down in two bites. He licked lips and said quietly, "Mom says chocolate is poison."

"And you listen to her?" A fleck of chocolate flew out of my mouth when I spoke.

"Only when she's around." Jake grinned shyly. "But we never have it in the house. At Halloween, she hands out raisins."

"I feel your pain." Michael snapped his bar in two and gave half to Jake. "Here, you better have this. You've got a lot of catching up to do."

I bit another square from mine, flattened it against the top of my mouth and waited for it to dissolve. Waiting. I had spent most of my life waiting for something in another moment. Waiting to be old enough to go to school. Waiting for the next hockey game. Waiting for Friday nights. Waiting for popcorn to pop. For once in my life all I needed to think was now, this exact minute. With no phone, no Wi-Fi, and no TV, there was only the present.

Michael eyed Jake's backpack. "What's in your pack, Jake?"

"Clothes 'n stuff."

"You went back into a totalled house for clothes? Didn't you bring enough last night?" Michael frowned.

"And his guitar." I pointed at the case beside the door. Then I stood and casually stretched my arms above my head. If I could convince Jake I wasn't worried, I could convince myself. "C'mon. You know where the basement is. Don't worry about Tony. As you saw last night he leaves us pretty much to ourselves down there."

I opened the screen door. After the earthquake and all the chaos outside, the living room seemed serene and inviting. It had an L-shaped sofa, a slow combustion stove, a large-screen TV set in the wall and a few paintings bolted to the gypsum board. Most people would have taken all that in and relaxed. Not Jake. He stopped and stared at the open door to Tony's office, the door that Tony usually kept closed. His face paled at the rows of CCTV monitors that tracked movement on every inch of the yard.

"Does he have cameras in your bedrooms?"

I snorted. "He's paranoid not a pervert. He just likes to see what's going on everywhere.

"I've never seen that in a house before."

"How many houses have you been in that are this modern?"

"Don't go into other houses much."

"What about your friends' places?" I wanted to know if he even had any friends. Jake's silence was a sad answer to my question.

I looked back and saw Michael's eyes widen in disbelief. I shrugged and thought about the way Jake's mom talked to him when she said goodbye the day before. She put her arm around his shoulders and got really close to his face, girlfriend close. Not that he had a girlfriend or much of a chance to get one as far as I could tell. I wondered who gave him the friendship bracelets he wore on his right wrist.

"I thought you homeschooled types met with other kids for sports and clubs and volunteer groups and stuff," I said as he bumped his backpack against the hallway wall on the way to Michael's room at the far end of the basement.

"Sometimes," Jake said quietly, like confessing something awful. I wondered why he didn't want to talk about his home-schooling and other kids he might know. One thing about learning to keep family business private was that I could sense when other people didn't want to talk about their personal lives. Maybe Jake would tell us more but not today. His voice was getting fainter every time he spoke.

Michael wheeled the trundle bed out of the TV room where Jake had slept the night before and into his room. He waved his arm in a big gesture. "You might be here for a while so *mi casa es su casa.*"

"That means my house is your house, or our house is your house," I translated.

Jake answered in a torrent of quiet Spanish that ended with, "*Iqualmente, si tuviera una casa.*"

I shook my head at him, and he repeated the last sentence a little slower and louder in case that helped me understand. Finally he muttered, "The same to you, if I still had a house." He turned away from me, embarrassed, as if I'd tricked him into speaking Spanish.

What else was hidden behind those nervous brown eyes?

The trundle bed was pushed against the desk on the far wall. "Your king-sized bed, sir. No one has slept in it since your last stay at Chez Morgan," Michael said.

Jake rubbed his nose. "Thanks."

"I'll bring you down some dinner later. I'm always eating so Tony won't think twice about it. Keep the blinds closed. I never let natural light in. I've got stacks of comics in boxes in the back of my closet if you want to read them." Jake looked at the laptop on the desk. Before he could ask, Michael said, "We're not allowed to turn on any computers when we're off the power grid. Here—" Michael reached into the bottom drawer of his bedside table. "This is a hand-crank flashlight. It's not much but it's the best I can offer. There's a deck of cards in the top drawer of my desk and a Rubik's cube. Don't worry; your mom should be home soon."

Jake nodded mutely.

He seemed to be fading fast so I cleared my throat to see how awake he was. "Remember the bathroom is a Jack and Jill to my bedroom so make sure you lock the door if you're in there. I don't want to get any unpleasant surprises." I looked at Jake to see if he knew I was teasing. His face gave no clues so I kept shovelling words into the vacuum. "Most people will have very little water. You've seen the rainwater tanks in our yard so you know we'll be okay. The toilets are composting so they're still working. Just be as quiet as you can. We don't want Tony hearing anything down here if the three of us are upstairs."

"Need to lie down," Jake said and crumpled onto the trundle bed, fully clothed. By the time his head touched the mattress he was asleep. I crouched and eased off his shoes. Michael covered him with a sheet and slid a pillow under his head.

"I know five-year-olds who take care of themselves better." I scowled at Jake and tried to remember any time in my life when I was as helpless as he was—when I had been allowed to be as helpless as he was. I couldn't remember back that far and I envied the simplicity of his life. I bet he never had to clean a bathroom or do a million loads of laundry in a single afternoon.

As Michael closed the door behind us, a loud noise outside, crowd noise, rushed in. We exchanged a glance and tore up the stairs, two at a time, to the front porch where we saw a small group, all male, surging around the gate. I counted five on the outside of the fence and only Michael and me on the inside. I hoped Jake would keep sleeping. He'd be worse than useless in all this.

Three of the agitators wore sunglasses, but the two who didn't had hard eyes, as dark as nightmares. They were about my age, maybe a bit older, and feral looking. I recognized a couple of guys from the local gang, Green Death. Everyone in the Valley knew the tags they spray-painted on anything that didn't move. One night they even tagged a row of cars sitting outside the police station on East Fourteenth. Nothing scared them, and I watched as the kid with red hair and a barcode tattoo on his cheek climbed halfway up the fence. I wanted to run inside and lock the door but I forced myself to stay there, head high. As my gut twisted into knots, I reminded myself how strong and brave I was. A few neighbours and other people gathered behind the gang. They hovered like vultures waiting to feed off someone else's kill.

CHAPTER 8 | MOB CONTROL

NORTH VANCOUVER

The neighbours knew Tony was the crazy survivalist guy because he was always telling them that they should be prepared for a disaster or a state of emergency. Last year he got the email addresses of everyone on the entire street and sent them all a link to a website that told them how to calculate emergency food rations. He stuck a copy of it on his kitchen bulletin board so that Michael and I could read it. Tony sent the email, not because he cared about people, but because he didn't want freeloaders showing up on his doorstep when the big one hit. It didn't take a genius to figure out that he was building his own food reserves. I bet everyone thought we were sitting on a gold mine. I wondered how the gang members found out but with the whole neighbourhood living free-range now, people were probably gossiping like crazy about Tony and his stash.

Michael trotted down the stairs, loose-limbed and casual. He walked to the gate. "Lose something?"

A tall dude with a scar from the side of his mouth to his ear steamrolled forward. The sun shimmered on his shaved head and showed all the flaws. It looked like an orange from the bottom of the bag, flat in some places, bulging in others. "We heard you've got a safe house. And supplies." He gestured to the rest of the gang and then to the neighbours setting up camps on their front lawns. "We need food and water and a kind of community gathering place. We figured your house would do just fine." His tone was sickly sweet, as if he was only thinking of others, but his real intent simmered beneath the surface. He wanted what we had and sharing with the needy wasn't part of his plan.

"Sorry, no room at the inn." Michael folded his arms.

"It's a big house." Scarface scowled at us.

"Yeah. It is. And it's full. Your friend may want to hop off the fence, we're about to turn on the electricity." Michael looked back at me and signalled yes.

The ferals edged back a bit. They talked between themselves, glared at Michael and then at me. Red hung on like he didn't believe Michael. I stepped into the house and flipped the power switch. Red's scream reached me inside Tony's office. When I went out again he was waving his hands. "You prick. You're a dead man."

He turned his hate-filled face my way and jabbed a finger at me. "And when I get hold of you, you're going to wish you was dead." Acid filled my mouth and my breathing fell shallow and low. He spat into his hands and flapped them as if he had third degree burns. I made contempt replace my fear. When Tony set up the fence, he got both Michael and me to feel the shock so we'd be willing to use it if necessary. It gave short, sharp pulses of electricity, meant to scare people, not hurt them.

I was glad that Red was such a wimp. It made me less afraid of him, like I'd seen him naked or something. He and his gang rumbled away, cursing and throwing dirty looks back at us. Everyone else wandered off. For the moment.

"You were warned," Michael shouted after them. "Go to the community centre or one of the schools. That's where the shelters are."

"That was lucky," I said when he came up the stairs.

He gasped a bit. "That wasn't luck. That was Tony's good planning."

The guys walked down the street and we heard their boiling over anger. Two houses away the Redgraves, Don and Cindy, talked with their heads close together. When they glowered at us, I waved and smiled. I guessed that they weren't talking about what outstanding citizens we were. Michael stayed silent. *Plan: fight fear with action. Stay busy.* I ran my fingers through my tangled, muddy hair. "I'm going to grab a shower. Then maybe the laundry fairy will get us all some clean clothes."

Michael nodded and his worried face loosened just a little. I walked to the basement on rubbery legs. Laundry. As if it was a normal day. What was Tony thinking? But maybe if I kept doing ordinary things in ordinary ways, our old life would slowly come back to us. I could pick beans and make dinner like it was an ordinary Wednesday. Perhaps then the power would come on again and the sirens would stop and our neighbours would get food at the supermarket again.

Then I thought about the houses outside the compound. About all the broken glass and shattered windows. How many houses and apartments were there in Vancouver? How many broken windows? How much glass would it take to fix that one small part of the damage? Nothing was going to get back to normal soon. A shiver ran down my arms as I realized it just might get a whole lot worse before it got better.

As I undressed, I found the owl feather I'd picked up in the park, and smoothed it flat. I tacked it to my pin board and whispered a prayer for Mom and Oliver. Tears burned my throat when I thought of Oliver, mauled by a bear or drowning in a creek. Then I pinched myself hard and thought of other things, specifically the Kurtz's cat. Michael would understand about Misty. He loved animals too, and he wouldn't let one suffer if he could help it.

After showering I found my favourite T-shirt, a Christmas special with the word *peace* written across it in sloping letters, under the image of a dove. It was a present from Lexy, my best friend. Putting it on made me feel closer to her. She and her family were in Europe. Had she heard of the Vancouver earthquake in the south of France? I missed the sound of her bubbly laugh. She was two inches taller than me and almost thirty pounds heavier. The big T-shirt slid over my shoulders and hung to my hips. Lexy bought me clothes in her size because that way if I didn't like them, she could have them back. This T-shirt would have looked great on her, but I told her it looked better on me. I wished she were here now so we could joke about that like we always did. She felt as far away as the stars.

I sorted laundry and started the washer and thought about Mom. I told myself that she'd be okay because she wouldn't be alone. Not that I knew that for sure but Mom had about a kajillion friends and was always surrounded by them. She was the people-person in the family. She had planned to hike the West Coast Trail again this month, between work trips into the mountains. Only I couldn't remember exactly what day. Was she on the trail when the quake hit? Had she been swept away by a tsunami? As soon as the thought fluttered into my head, I wished I could delete it. Please, please, please let her be safe.

What about Oliver, where was he? Every time I turned around I half expected to see him behind me. Wiggling his eyebrows. Tilting his head in hope of a game, a hug, or a treat. He couldn't be hurt. He just couldn't. I conjured him at my feet, shadowing me like he had since the first day I got him. I imagined the popcorn smell of his paws. I could hear the funny way he whimpered when he dreamed. I pushed away all worries of him injured or worse. *Oliver, come home.*

I found Michael lounged across the sofa in the TV room. His lip had stopped bleeding. Wet hair draped around his ears and the smell of his ginseng shampoo hung in a cloud around him. He wore only Hurley board shorts, leftovers from one of Tony's Hawaiian vacations. With his tanned six-pack he could have been an ad for a gym. He was reading *A Feast for Crows* and chewing an apple down to its stem.

"I thought I might go back to the forest. Try and find Oliver," I said.

He slammed his book shut. "No way. If I let you do that, Tony'd *kill* me."

"But Oliver could be hurt or hungry. I can't just leave him out there."

"Yeah, you can. You have to. Don't fight me on this. You're not going to win. I'm not letting you out that gate twice. Pirates' Code and all that."

I nodded. I had only caught one of Michael's secrets. That only allowed me only one favour. I couldn't argue with the code because I wrote it. But I could try reason. "C'mon, Michael, we've got to get Oliver back."

"Why? He's a smart little dog. Even if he's hurt, he'll find his way home. He's probably just resting somewhere, getting over the shock of the earthquake. Like you and I should be doing before Tony gets back with more jobs." His voice quavered and worry drifted across his face. He was more rattled than I realized.

Michael looked over my shoulder as Jake stepped out of the bedroom. He wore jeans and a black Moxy Früvous T-shirt. He didn't say anything, just stood and listened, like a ghost.

I turned back to Michael. "I have to go and feed Misty."

"You don't *have* to feed Misty."

"Yes I *do*. She'll starve if I don't go."

"Let her catch mice for a day or two. You can't leave the compound for a freaking cat. Case closed." He stood, put his hands on his hips, and started doing trunk twists.

"She's locked in the Kurtzes' garage. There aren't any mice there. She probably doesn't have any water. I'll bring her back here and then I won't have to go out again, okay?" I didn't say that if I could help Misty then cosmic goodness would get Oliver back to me safe. If I went on a mission of mercy, I might find Oliver on the short walk from our house to Misty's. I imagined him running down the street, nose to the ground, and tail wagging. I didn't say any of that to Michael because he didn't believe in cosmic forces. He was studying to be an engineer, which meant he was learning to measure everything.

"What if the gang members come back or the neighbours try to rush the place?" He rotated left, then right.

"Jake could sit look out."

"And if Tony comes home?"

"He's been gone, how long? An hour? He won't be back for a while yet. Plenty of time to get down the street and back."

Michael dropped his hands to his sides and stood still. He was starting to cave so I said, "Besides, if you promised to take care of someone or something, wouldn't you do your very best to keep that promise?"

"Fine." Michael sighed. "But I'm not letting you go by yourself. And she stays in your room until the Kurtzes get back."

"I'm allergic to cats," Jake said.

I whirled around and smoked him with my eyes. "Well stay out of my bedroom then."

Jake's body sagged. Once again I hated myself. Being a Good Samaritan was a hard act to sustain.

When Michael and I were sure that the gang was gone, we slipped out and walked quickly down the street. Cracks big enough to swallow small animals split the road and the smell of burning wood clogged the air. I pretended not to see the worried glances from the neighbours. An announcer's voice reached me from someone's tinny radio. "All hospitals are operational with only superficial damage. However emergency facilities are overflowing. Triage is being done to determine the most severe injuries at this time."

The words blackened my thoughts. I realized a lot of what Tony predicted had already started to come true. How long would it be before more stressed, hungry people were knocking on our door for help? How much help could we offer? What would Tony's rules be then?

I watched the entrance to the cul-de-sac. For all my brave talk in front of Jake, I seriously did not want to fight with the old man. I planned my defence. Misty was my responsibility this week and Morgans honour their commitments. Therefore I was on a mission of honour, at the very least, a duty mission. Satisfied that my logic would stand up in the Supreme Court of Tony, I looked closer at the Kurtz house.

The aftershocks had knocked more bricks out of the front wall. Only the new double garage seemed sound. I unlocked the door and peered into the empty cavern. A trail of bloody paw prints led through the broken glass from the windows to outside and I straightened my shoulders. I couldn't let Michael see me worried. "Let's take all the cat food, in case they don't get back this weekend."

"You think that's a possibility, do you?" Worry scraped the edge of Michael's voice.

"Mikey, we're going to be okay I just know we are. And I know that Mom's okay too. I bet they'll bring the army in and get things fixed up in no time," I said with false confidence and used his childhood nickname to be extra comforting. When he smiled slightly, it filled me with fresh confidence in our ability to get through this together.

I picked up the cat carrier and he loaded cat supplies into a canvas bag. "I hope so, Row, I really do. But I don't know what's going on..."

A weak meow bleated in the yard. Michael pointed to the flowers beside the patio and stood statue-still. I crept outside slowly and sat down on a cracked paving stone. Flat smudges of blood led to the flowerbed. I reminded myself that Misty didn't like to be picked up. If she was hurt, she'd be more nervous than ever. With my softest voice I repeated her name a few times and ended with, "C'mon, puss."

I waited and waited. Just when I was ready to give up she shook herself free of the flowers and limped over to me. I ignored her and she lay down on the warm concrete beside me and curled into the letter *S*. As I reached to touch her, an aftershock vibrated the ground. She jumped to her feet but I was too fast; I pinned her by her neck.

As I pushed Misty into the carrier, she fought back, claws bared. With a protesting yowl, she raked my hand. The pain was sharp and immediate. Four parallel tracks oozed blood.

"That's it," I swore as I licked the wound. "I'm not helping anyone else."

CHAPTER 9 | AFTERSHOCKS

VANCOUVER, WEST END

White-hot pain singed Dixie Morgan awake. She blinked into the surrounding blackness and tried to remember where she was. The vague memory of cycling past the glittering water of Kitsilano Beach surfaced. *Who was with me? Tony? Not Tony. Haven't ridden with him since the kids were little.* She opened her eyes wide but saw only darkness. *I'm not blind. It is dark here. But where is here?*

Something heavy pinned her right leg and she lay with her face pressed into the gritty tile floor. She coughed, spat out a mouthful of dust, and raised her head. Fresh air seeped in from beyond the darkness and sparked her hope.

Her shoulder twinged and she stretched her arms but found she couldn't quite straighten them. Instead her fingers fumbled against what felt like a concrete block. When she arched her back, her head struck a metal girder and made a dull thudding noise. She moaned hoarsely and collapsed back into unconsciousness.

Hours later she woke again, determined to free herself. She flexed her left leg and foot and sighed with relief. *Now the right one.* She tensed her core, exhaled, and tried to wrench herself free. Savage pain swamped her and her leg didn't budge. *Trapped. I'm part of the building now.* Terrifying memories rushed back and she shuddered with dread. *An earthquake. Yes that was it.*

VANCOUVER, DOWNTOWN

When the tremors ended, Linda Patterson heard the other hotel guest count to ten slowly. He crawled out from under his chair and Linda sat, dazed, looking around the reception lounge.

"Mrs. Patterson, are you okay?" The receptionist's head rose slowly from the other side of the desk. Her magenta lipstick was smeared. Underneath the dark tan her complexion had paled.

Linda stood and brushed herself off. Dust floated out of the walls and ceiling like gritty snow. She gazed up at the receptionist and forced herself to stay calm. "I'm fine. What about you? You okay?"

"Yeah," she whispered. The tears that rolled down her cheeks made her appear young and vulnerable.

Linda said, "Good. Now I've got to get home to my son. He'll be frantically worried about me." She was sure the receptionist didn't care about her or her son but she needed to say something normal to someone.

The man who had helped her was dusting off his pants. "I need to get home, too," he said. "I live in Calgary. Do you suppose the airport is still open?"

Linda shook her head blankly and pointed her chin at the buckled columns in the hotel lobby. "Whatever we do, we'd better get out of here fast," she said.

She snatched her purse and overnight bag and ran down the two flights of stairs to the parking lot. The fire door was warped shut in its frame, and a stocky cyclist was trying to force it open with his shoulder.

"Stand back!" she said, and hurled her overnight bag at the glass door with all her strength. The first blow cracked the tempered glass but it bounced off. The cyclist picked up the bag and, with a mighty heave, drove it through the door. Linda thought she'd never heard such a sweet sound as that glass shattering.

"After you," the man said and stood back. Dazed, Linda stepped into the parking lot. Into the first circle of hell. The ceiling had collapsed. Somewhere in that mountain of busted concrete and twisted steel was her pale blue BMW.

CHAPTER 10 | MICHAEL IN CHARGE

NORTH VANCOUVER

If I'd known Tony was going to take so long I would've eaten a snack with the guys at our regular dinnertime. Only Tony liked us to eat together and after breaking his stay-inside rule twice in the first hour he was gone, I wanted to be on his good side. At five, Michael had another of his cold cut specials and I'd taken Jake another cheese sandwich. His nose twitched like a rabbit as he chewed and I left it with him so I wouldn't have to watch. By the time Tony's pickup drove up to the gate, it was nearly sunset. I was ready to gnaw my own arm off.

But when Michael opened the gate, it wasn't Tony who drove into the yard. Javier slouched behind the wheel for a minute before he slid out. His face was drawn. He wore a tattered T-shirt and jeans cut off at the knee. Every inch of his clothing and skin was splattered with blood. Dried blood even dotted his thick salt-and-pepper hair.

"Where's Tony?" Michael said, easing the gate shut. I braced myself at the bottom of the steps. I felt the bad news before it punched me in the gut.

Javier swiped off his sunglasses with a trembling hand. His eyes were red and tired looking. He said quickly, "There's been an accident."

"What type of accident?" I said. Fear almost choked me silent.

"A shooting accident."

The smell of blood from his clothing stuck in my throat. I held my breath.

"Where's Tony?" Michael asked in a high, thin voice.

Javier flung out his answer like a single long word. "He's-at-the-hospital-he's-got-a-bed-and-I-left-him-in-the-hands-of-a-very-capable nurse."

I exhaled.

"What happened?" Michael wound the key lanyard around his fingers before scrunching it into a ball.

"After we shot the deer, our pain-in-the-ass next door neighbours came over and started bitching about firearms in the suburbs. Tony gave the rifle to LJ to clean and put away but LJ stashed it behind the back steps because he wanted to see the fight with the neighbours. When they finally got off our backs no one was thinking about the gun any longer. We were talking about how they had no idea how scarce food might get. The next thing we knew, Alex picked the gun up and pointed it at Tony. He thought it was a toy. I yelled at him to put it down but he panicked and pulled the trigger." Javier's light Spanish accent softened the rapid words but not the message. I thought of Javier's youngest son Alex. How old was he now? Five? Six? Copying the men with the guns. And LJ—little Javier—he was only about thirteen himself. Why were the guns anywhere near them?

"Where'd he hit him?" Michael's voice hitched.

A mosquito landed on my wrist and I smacked it dead. When I flicked its flattened body away it left a trail of blood across my skin.

"In the left arm, but it went straight through the flesh. Missed the bone. The main thing is he lost a lot of blood." Javier's speech slowed and his round body deflated.

My head swam and I rubbed at the mosquito bite. "Alexander shot Tony," I said more to myself than anyone else.

"He's going to be okay." Javier's tone lifted and he almost sounded okay again but I'd seen behind his mask and I knew he was worried. He tried to sound reassuring but he'd started to sweat hard. "We got him to the best place possible. To the hospital."

"Cypress Grove?"

"Yes," Javier said a little impatiently. "Both bridges are closed. I couldn't exactly take him downtown, could I?"

"Is the hospital really okay?" I thought about the radio reports in the afternoon. "They can look after him? How long will he be there?

"Yep, the hospital is okay. Lots of emergency workers on hand. Your old man lost a lot of blood so I don't know how long they'll keep him—a couple of days at least," he said with a tense smile. "I tell you, getting to the ER wasn't easy. All the roads around it are torn up, caved in. Houses and apartment buildings are down, blocking the way. It's a mess. I drove as close as I could. Then we walked the last two blocks." He shook his head as if he couldn't believe they'd made it.

My mind spun into overdrive. "But he needs clean clothes and his razor and...and...and what about all his vitamins? He needs those. He says all that crap keeps him strong." Thoughts tumbled out of my mouth. "We'd better go see him and take him his stuff."

"No. Tony said to tell you to stay here. Don't leave the property." Javier waved away my idea. "His orders. Get a bag together for him and I'll pick it up tomorrow and take it over. Then I'll come back here and give you a full report."

Michael twisted the lanyard. "When did all this happen?"

Javier checked his watch. "Five hours ago? A little longer. It took a while to get someone to pay attention to us at the hospital. Then I stopped at my place to see how everybody was doing there."

"Tony walked two blocks?" He couldn't have been too badly injured if he walked. Another mosquito buzzed around my face and I crushed it on my neck.

"Yeah. Not fast but he got there. He told them it was an accident, a self-inflicted wound so there wouldn't be too many questions. Not that they were too particular today. They had a lot of incoming." Javier paused. "Anyway, he said to tell you, Michael is commanding officer. No one is to enter or leave this compound other than me. Got it?"

"No. No, I don't have it!" My anger boiled over. "Tony's injured and we can't see him? God!"

Michael squared his shoulders. "Rowan's right. We need to see him."

Javier shook his head. "Out of the question. Tony said to remind you about chain of command. His orders were clear. You're to stay here and protect the place. Stay out of trouble."

I was speechless. How could they have left a loaded weapon around with three young boys in the yard? Didn't they know anything about gun safety? *Gun safety.* What an oxymoron. No wonder Javier's wife Tammi made him keep his gun at Tony's house. If he kept them at his place, his whole family'd probably be dead by now.

Javier dragged the gun case out of the car. "It's already cleaned so let's put it away."

I followed him and Michael around the side of the house to the laundry room where Michael went to the cupboard with the false back. He opened the safe, put the gun case in, and spun the tumblers.

When the safe was locked again, Michael and Javier just stood looking at each other for a minute. It was like they were having a silent prayer meeting together, they were both so intense.

Michael spoke first, "Thanks for taking care of Tony. You've always got our backs. Anything we can do to help you and your family?"

My jaw dropped but neither of them noticed. Was he inviting Javier and the whole Rodrigues family to move in with us? Javier's eyes glistened. "Michael, you are a credit to your father. Our home is secure and we have good food supplies."

He paused for a minute as if he was imagining his house. He shook his head slightly. "The boys are upset about everything, the quake, the injured deer, Alex shooting Tony. Alex hasn't stopped crying since the accident." Javier swallowed. "The only thing is water. I was going to restock our supplies but I never got around to it. We've been so prepared for so long, I just thought it wasn't so important any longer. I thought the quake was never going to happen."

Michael said. "You've always been there when I had things that I couldn't take to Tony. This is my chance to help you. You know we've got lots of water in our tanks so I'm pretty certain we won't need the bottled water too. Come and see Aladdin's cave."

Just like that Michael took the key from its hiding spot behind the washer and unlocked that door to the steep stairs that led down to Tony's doomsday cache. He put his hand on Javier's shoulder and said, "*Mi casa es su casa.*"

Without a word, Javier followed him into the hidden cellar that I knew by heart: a large freezer ran the length of one wall. The other three walls were fitted with shelves from the floor to the ceiling. One entire wall was stacked with every type of canned and dried food that could be bought in bulk. Along another wall, mason jars of home preserves were lined up in order of date and food type. I'd memorized it during all the times I'd stacked shelves and done stock rotation with Tony. Still it was meant to be top secret, only known by family members. I chewed my lip and sorted the sun-dried laundry.

Being an honorary uncle made Javier family, I decided. Tony and he had fished and hunted together for years. Sometimes Tony called Javier "the little brother I never had" and I'd always referred to him as Uncle Javier. But Javier hadn't followed Tony's rule about preparation or he wouldn't need any of our stuff. Maybe Tony was always on my case for a reason. He wanted me to be ready for the worst, even if others weren't.

When they emerged, the deep furrows in Javier's face had softened and he didn't look quite so lost. He carried a flat of water under each arm. "Thanks," he said. "You're a true friend."

"Seriously, Uncle Javier, we'll be fine. You can trust me, you know that, don't you?" Michael looked into Javier's dark brown eyes. A spark of affection fired between them. Their bond was formed before I was born, before Javier had sons of his own.

"I hope my boys turn out as well as you have. I can't believe you've got another full scholarship this year," Javier said that like it was a fresh bulletin, like it wasn't this summer's endless news loop.

I trailed behind them to the gate thinking about how disasters were supposed to bring people together. Somehow it felt like Michael and Javier were pushing me away from the fire, from the warmth of their special friendship. I thought about the bright green Kawasaki and wished I'd bought it when I had the chance. Then I'd get on it and ride to some place safe and friendly, away from these guys and their secret handshakes. As if he read my thoughts, Javier stopped, put down a flat of water and hugged me with one arm. He smelled of sweat and blood. His unshaved face rubbed sandpaper-rough against my cheek. I stepped away and he shook hands with Michael. Then he pulled him close and held him for a minute. When they broke apart, Javier slipped into the street. He called over his shoulder, "Be strong. Tony is counting on you to look after this place. Keep it ready for when he comes home."

I waited until Javier was at the end of the cul-de-sac. Michael and I retreated to the porch, and I chose my words carefully. "Was it my imagination or did he seem more worried than he let on?"

"He seemed deeply worried."

"About Tony d'you think?"

"No, not so much about Tony. He's in the hospital and was probably in one of the first waves of casualties brought in so I'm guessing he got lots of attention, way more than if he'd been hurt now. Tony'll be okay." Michael trotted up the front stairs and I followed. "But Uncle Javier's got a lot to worry about. You know how young his kids are. I had to help him for their sake."

"Understood. I think Tony might've done the same. But it looks like things are pretty bad out there. Maybe Tony had a reason for wanting to hang onto what he's got stored here."

"Javier's Tony's best friend," Michael said like that was the end of the discussion. He stretched across the plastic loveseat.

I sat in the rocker, rubbing the smooth wood of the armrests with my hands. "Fine. But there are two of us here, guarding the fort. How about in future we talk about who we give stuff too. You know, keep it democratic?"

"Don't think so. I'm in charge so I'll make the decisions. For the last couple of years, Uncle Javier's been more of a father to me than Tony has. He doesn't expect me to live my life for him."

"Forget Uncle Javier. He's your friend. I get that. He's also the closest to family that we have in Vancouver. But what about other people? Who else might we want to help that Tony might not agree with? We've got to make some decisions together, especially big ones like giving stuff away."

"Not according to Tony." He grinned. "I was only second-in-command before. Now I'm the boss, little sister. Get used to it."

I didn't want to see his smug face so I marched down the stairs to the back yard and checked on the chickens. One grey straggler pecked away at the dirt, making low gurgling noises in her throat. The others had already settled into the house for the night and with a little nudge, the last hen joined them. I closed the door and locked them into their safe little world.

I needed time alone to think. Always happy Javier was anxious and tense. I'd known him my entire life and never seen him zoned-out and troubled like tonight. I worried about what Javier wasn't saying, about Tony and everything else on the outside. Seeing him fearful was seeing the world turned upside down. But I was ready for that upheaval; Tony had helped me prepare. Now Tony wasn't there to watch me and it seemed more important than ever to learn from what he had taught me.

Only 8:15 and there wasn't much light left. The days were shrinking fast and an occasional yellow leaf floated down like the first snow. Soon the birds would disappear with the warm sunshine. There'd be nothing ahead but winter's darkness. Summer was dying. What was dying with it?

CHAPTER 11 | HOMEWARD BOUND

VANCOUVER, EAST SIDE

Two hours after driving her overnight bag through the glass door, Linda Patterson was part of a slow-moving crowd on Hastings Street. People, some injured and bloody-faced, made their way around the abandoned vehicles and ruptures in the road. Many moved like they were hypnotized, following the crowd listlessly, not speaking. A crew from a solitary fire engine waged war on flames engulfing a low-rise building. An elderly couple on the third floor clung to the railing of a deck that listed at a precarious angle. Their pleas for help barely registered as Linda walked past.

She stared at the two teenaged girls in front of her. They wore tiny halter-tops, brief shorts, and flip-flops. As they sauntered along, flaunting their taut young bodies, they passed a joint back and forth. They laughed and pointed at things as if they were at a sideshow. The sticky smell of marijuana trailed on the air behind them. One girl pushed a bicycle.

Linda walked a little faster. "May I borrow your bike?" she asked.

The bike owner tossed back her light brown bangs, the same way Rowan Morgan did. Linda tried to conceal her dislike of the gesture, of teenaged girls in general. The girl looked at her friend and smirked. "Borrow?" she said with heavy sarcasm. "Like you're going to give it back to me in five minutes?"

Linda could only think of one thing, getting to Jacob. Cars couldn't travel these congested streets. It would take hours to walk home. She needed that bike. "Do you want to sell it?" she asked.

"I might," the girl said. "How much you got?"

Linda rifled through her wallet. "One hundred and twenty dollars?"

"You're joking, right?" The girl rolled her eyes. She and her friend turned to go, the same way Rowan had walked away the day before when Linda had tried to explain the reasons Jacob shouldn't go into the forest. Stifling her rising temper, Linda studied her hands, at the gifts from her husband.

"How about my watch? It's a Cartier. Worth thousands." She hoped she didn't sound as desperate as she felt.

The girl's friend pushed the long black hair off her face and lifted Linda's wrist. "Watches are for oldsters. But that rock looks fine." She grinned slyly and passed Linda's hand to Bicycle Girl for closer inspection. Linda cringed. The two-carat diamond was the most valuable thing she owned.

"Are you kidding? It's a zircon and probably not worth as much as your flip-flops. What about my necklace? These are real diamonds and worth a fortune. Or my bracelets?" Linda yanked the gold bangles off her wrists. "Eighteen-carat, worth as much as the necklace. Take the necklace *and* the bracelets?"

Bicycle Girl scowled. "Nope. The ring. That or I keep the bike."

Linda's chest pounded as she wrestled the ring off her finger. She dropped it in the girl's hand and snatched the bike away. When she jumped on it, BMX skills from her childhood erupted deep in her brain. She navigated the mangled streets and dense crowds with fierce concentration, ignoring the misery around her. She couldn't help anyone; her job was to get home, to find Jacob.

As the crowd turned the corner to the last approach to the Ironworkers' Memorial Bridge, it came to a near standstill. Linda dismounted and nudged the bike forward, around the stragglers and the family groups. People surged and shifted in front of four police officers who stood on the hoods and roofs or their cruisers. One young cop spoke into a megaphone. "Stay back. The bridge isn't safe." Even from a distance, Linda heard the worry in his voice. He shouted into his bullhorn. "Engineers have to certify the soundness of the bridge before anyone crosses."

The ground started to shake again. A single howl rose from a thousand throats. The policeman fell from his perch. The tremor stopped and the mob roared. The crowd boiled forward and in the next second Linda saw two lightweight traffic barriers being thrown over the side of the bridge. She pushed forward, past a father with two distraught toddlers, past an old woman with a cane, past a troop of office workers wearing dust masks.

With energy she hadn't felt since adolescence, she forced her way to the front of the shoving horde. She swung her leg over the bike and rode with the fury of a woman possessed.

CHAPTER 12 | HOME ALONE

NORTH VANCOUVER

Michael and I prepared dinner together on autopilot and a quiet peace settled between us. I wanted to be alone with Michael and I guess he felt the same because he didn't say a word about Jake. We went about the rituals of slicing zucchini and potatoes and marinating steaks. For a few precious minutes it was as if the world hadn't changed and my worries faded.

When everything was ready, I found Jake reading comics with a flashlight. The hot, airless room smelled of bubble gum and he still wore the paramedic hoodie. He looked up at me. "Have you got any art supplies?"

"What?" I reminded myself that he didn't know Tony was hurt.

"I've got an idea for a graphic novel."

"Guess what? You won't have to find ways to fill in your time any longer. Tony's in the hospital. The three of us are alone here and you can help us take care of the place."

Jake dropped his head and rubbed his nose. His hair covered his face again. "Um. Good. I guess."

"No. Not good, Jake. Not good at all. He's been shot! His moron best friend left a loaded rifle where his kid picked it up."

"What?" Jake rubbed his nose. "Sorry, I didn't know...."

"Forget it. C'mon up. Dinner's ready."

In the kitchen Jake sat and didn't speak. Maybe he was afraid of saying the wrong thing again. I knew that feeling well. Michael brought three plates in from the deck. He set them down in front of us and Jake said quietly, "I'm vegetarian."

"Forgot. Sorry." I reached over and picked the meat off his plate with my fingers. "Well it hasn't touched the vegetables so you won't die. But the barbecue is our main way of cooking for now. You can deal with that or go hungry." I sank my teeth into a chunk of meat and glared at Jake. There was something tight and hard in my stomach and I didn't want to eat at all but I knew I had to. I had to stay strong for whatever came next.

Jake hung his head, like I'd slapped him or something, and I felt about two inches tall. I wasn't really mad at him. I was worried about Mom and Tony and Oliver and everyone else. He just happened to wander into my line of fire.

After that the only sound in the room was eating and cutlery clanking. Once I watched a documentary about lions in the Serengeti and it showed them feeding on a dead zebra. As the lions ate, they made low murmuring noises. Michael and Jake made those same noises as they attacked their dinners, sounds of contentment. I was in the African veldt, surrounded by wild animals. I ate silently and tried to close my ears, which is just about impossible so I hummed a little as I chewed. When Michael was finished he pushed his plate away with a loud belch. Then he stood and crooked his finger at Jake. "Let's get out there and finish stringing the razor wire along the top of the fence."

Jake's face whitened and I felt sorry for him.

"It's dark out," he said.

"Yep, and the house is surrounded by automatic, ultra-bright security lighting. It'll be like working in the middle of the day." Michael said.

"Is that really necessary?" I said. "I mean can't it wait until Tony gets home?"

"I'm guessing if he's got a shot-up arm, he's not going to be good for a whole lot of that type of work for a while. Also that scene outside today proves that he was right about the quake. So just in case he's right about other things, like food and water shortages, then yeah, I think we better keep Fortress Tony as secure as we can. Better to be prepared and not need it than the other way around, right?" That last part sounded exactly like Tony. I set my jaw at his bossy tone.

"I'm not touching that stuff." I wrapped my ponytail around my fingers and studied each strand of hair for split ends.

"No, you're doing kitchen clean up. In the meantime, Jake, you and me've got to put on some heavy gloves and thick jackets. The old man says stringing razor wire is like making love to a porcupine. You have to do it carefully." He laughed. "Don't worry, I got it half finished. We'll be done in no time."

Job completed, Michael climbed the front stairs and tossed his gloves into a heap by the door. He took a long drink of water and Jake copied him. He put his hand on his hip, the same way Michael did. It was as if working together made them members of the fraternal order of razor-wire engineers. I rocked in Tony's chair. Michael sat next to me and Jake took the seat nearest the door. Outside the compound the four Redgrave boys made ghostly shadows as they darted around people's campfires and makeshift shelters, shrieking and throwing a football back and forth.

"Why're those people camping on their lawns? Their places aren't trashed like mine?" Jake spoke with fire and the slight hint of anger changed him somehow. For a fleeting moment he was made of spark and fight. I liked him better that way.

"I'm guessing that a lot of people are way worse off than you, Jake." Michael took a small radio out of his jeans pocket. "While Jake read comics and you played with the cat this afternoon, I listened to the news reports."

"Turn it on," I said.

"No." Michael flicked his head toward Jake and I caught his message. Better not stir up new worries. Anxious people make bad decisions, take silly risks. Jake hadn't mentioned his mom for a while but he kept peering toward the pathway that joined our two houses, as if he expected her to come walking over to our place at any minute.

"What I've heard so far is that a lot of buildings are down. Tons of people are dead or missing. Sinkholes are forming all over the place. Fires are burning everywhere, the SkyTrain line crumbled in half a dozen places. No phones anywhere." Michael was repeating the tip-of-the-iceberg news from what he'd heard on the radio and I knew it. Michael and I were prepared for what was out there, on one level anyway. Jake wasn't and if he were to start to imagine how huge the disaster was, he might start ripping out his hair. As it was, he ran his fingers through it about once a minute. It was nice hair too. Thick, almost black, and just a little wavy.

Against the night sky distant fires glowed. We heard an occasional faraway siren. It felt like we were shipwrecked on an island. We were safe, but for how long?

"There aren't many sirens," Jake said after a while.

"Lots of fires, not so much water to put them out, I'm guessing." Michael said.

Michael didn't mention ambulances. Maybe like me, he didn't want to think about them. Tony had walked two blocks with a bleeding wound. I didn't know where Mom and Mrs. Patterson were. What if one of them needed help and couldn't get it? Maybe paramedics didn't have to drive far to find people they could help. Maybe there was no point in hurrying them back to the hospital because everyone was overwhelmed.

Michael rested his jaw on his fist as if he shared my dark thoughts. It didn't register when Jake went into the house, letting the screen door slam behind him. A few minutes later he returned with three glasses, a litre of vodka, and a jumbo bottle of orange pop.

"Where'd you get that?" I said. Michael frowned.

"From your pantry." Jake grinned. I didn't realize he'd been paying so much attention to what was in our house.

"Are you crazy? Liquor is the last thing we need right now."

"You said your house is my house."

"Not alcohol though. In emergency situations, you shouldn't take anything that impairs your judgement." I quoted Tony and waited for Michael to support me.

Jake looked from me to Michael. Doubt flickered across Michael's face only for a second. Then he shrugged and took the glasses and vodka from Jake.

"Don't worry Rowan, no one's going to force you to drink if you don't want to. He slopped a generous amount of vodka in two glasses before filling all of them with orange soda. I took the glass of plain pop. Michael handed a glass to Jake. "Crazy times call for crazy measures. Maybe Jake and I just need a drink to relax a bit. We've both been pretty tense all day."

I chewed my lip. Alcohol changed Michael in ways I didn't like. It made him aggressive and kind of stupid. It turned him into someone I didn't know or trust.

Jake glanced at me, slightly apologetic, slightly defiant at the same time. Then he took a big slug. I think he wanted to prove something to me. That he was daring and smart? That he could party? I didn't know and I wished he'd found another way to show me whatever I was supposed to see.

"To surviving the big one." Michael raised his glass in salute. I pretended I was okay with what he was doing and touched my glass to his and Jake's. Jake drank half his in a single go. They smacked their lips as they drank and talked loudly about what a good job they'd done stringing the razor wire.

Let them have their party. I wanted to plan tomorrow and the day after that.

"I know what I want to do tomorrow," I said.

"Which is?" Michael sipped his drink without looking at me.

"I want to find Oliver."

"We'll see," Michael said. "That depends on a lot of things."

"Like?"

"If we are out of a state of emergency yet."

"In other words, no." My temper flared but I said nothing. *Stop. Think. Observe. Plan.* If Tony was right about major disasters, we could be holed up in this compound for weeks or longer. *When major infrastructure fails, it will be months before life returns to normal.* I thought about how my life be stuck inside with the friendly dictator. A plan hatched in my brain. I knew what I would do the next day. Me, myself, and I. As my idea took shape, the Muellers' car drove up the cul-de-sac. It reversed into their wide driveway and Mrs. Mueller got out of the driver's side. She helped the youngest out of his booster seat.

I turned to Michael. "I thought you said they went to Lismore High? That it was set up as an evacuation centre?"

He shrugged and picked at a barbed wire cut on the back of his hand. Blood started to trickle out of it again and he licked the crimson drops. Gross. "I think I'll go talk to them, get an idea of why they came back. You two can hit the sack. I'll sit up and keep watch like Tony wants us to. Rowan, you can relieve me around six in the morning."

"I'm not doing anything if I don't have a key to the gate," I said firmly. "I'm not going to be a prisoner here. I'm pretty sure that's illegal by the way."

Michael's eyes were locked on the action next door. The Mueller kids had scooped armfuls of pillows and sleeping bags out of the car. They were waiting for further instructions. Mr. and Mrs. Mueller looked at each other, at the house, and at each other again. *Why had they come back?* I jumped to my feet. "I'm coming with you. I want to hear what happened."

Jake stood up beside me and said, "Yeah, me too."

Michael threw up his hands. "I guess I know when I'm outnumbered."

Jake grinned slightly as if we'd just formed a secret alliance and I smiled back. We went through the gate single-file and Michael locked it behind us. I'd always felt self-conscious about what Mom called Tony's Infrastructure of Paranoia. The motion detector lights, the CCTV camera, a high chain-link fence. Totally over-the-top, she said. Was she right? Was it really over-the-top? What had kept the ferals out this afternoon? That very same infrastructure of paranoia.

As we neared the Muellers, I realized how lucky I was. At least one person in my family had planned for every contingency. Both of the adult Muellers looked like they had been dragged backwards through a wind tunnel. Their matching dyed blond hair stood on end. Their clothes were creased and stained. The three young children had the hollow-eyed faces of the homeless.

"How was Lismore High?" Michael asked.

"It was one disaster on top of another one," Mrs. Mueller hiccupped. To my embarrassment, I saw that she was crying, with the kids there and everything.

Mr. Mueller rubbed his neck with stubby fingers. "There were no cots or mattresses and the place was packed to the rafters. Absolutely no privacy and lots of people arguing, some crying. A few injured people and only one guy there with first aid training and very limited supplies. There was no one in charge and some people were holding spots for others who might never get there. That didn't stop them being junk-yard-dog mean when we tried to find space for our blankets. The clincher was when Chloe got pushed around by a couple of bigger kids on her way to the bathroom. Hailey was right behind her and tried to help her but the big kids went after her too. We decided we'd be better off sleeping here tonight than taking our chances there. We're going to sleep on the back deck."

"Okay, if you're really nervous about going inside that should work. First thing you need to do is dig a latrine pit in your back yard, as far from the house as possible." Michael sounded just like Tony giving orders.

Mr. Mueller nodded. The kids clung to Mrs. Mueller's dirty denim skirt like barnacles. For a moment I wondered if we should invite them into Fortress Tony as well. Then I remembered that the kids fought all the time, big physical fights. Besides it didn't matter what I thought when Tony's rules were clear on the subject. Michael was in charge, not me. I might was well just cut out my tongue.

Mrs. Mueller opened the gate to the back yard. "Hey, kids, who wants to have a sleepover on the back deck? Chloe honey, bring your flashlight." She went first and they followed like nervous ducklings.

Mr. Mueller waited until they were out of sight. He wiped his lips with the back of his hand. "There was a hydro worker at the school with his family. He said the lines are so badly damaged he doesn't think the power will be on for a month, if not longer. And it's going to be restored for essential services first."

His voice broke. Even though he always cheated me on my babysitting money, I felt a little sorry for him, but only a little. I felt sorrier for the kids because he should have been better prepared. Michael must have been feeling the same because he said, "Do you have the emergency water bags Tony gave you? We can spare a little water."

Mr. Mueller stared past us, gazing into space for the answer. He mumbled something.

"Beg your pardon?" Michael said.

"I'm sorry," Mr. Mueller said a little louder. "I never believed Tony. I only took the bags to get him off my back." He wiped his mouth again. "They're probably still there. Let me see."

I gawked at Michael, incredulous. Sure, just give it away. What happened to *we take care of family first. No one else.* Those were the last rules Tony laid down that afternoon. Maybe I'd bent them a bit, but only because I owed it to Jake and Misty to look after them.

If Michael was ready to give water to Javier and to the Muellers, why stop there? Why not give some to the Redgraves too? In fact why not just open the gate and let people in? The more I thought about what Michael was doing, the angrier I got. Mainly I was mad because I guessed Michael was being vodka-generous. Tony'd go apeshit when he found out.

Mr. Mueller rummaged through the front of the garage and found two twenty-litre water bags. Jake and I followed close to Michael and him. They spoke in quiet voices, but I heard *SeaBus swamped, people drowned* and something about an oil tanker floundering in Burrard Inlet.

Michael stopped outside the gate and handed the collapsible bags to Jake. "Please fill these from the tank in the back yard." He added, "Rowan, you'd better help him." Then he turned to back to Mr. Mueller. "We can't do this for everyone so please don't tell anyone where you got this water."

I trotted after Jake and whispered, "Did you hear what he said about the SeaBus?"

"Yeah," Jake said. "And he seemed really worried too."

Jake was right. Mr. Mueller was the second adult that night to be seriously anxious about what he'd seen on the outside. A pang of worry speared through me. "I wonder where our moms are."

"I don't know," Jake said. When I saw the worry in his eyes, I wished I hadn't brought up the subject. It's not as if he could do anything. He shuffled over to the rainwater tank but I shook my head.

"We've got way better water than that," I said. If we were going to help people, we'd do it right. I didn't want anyone, especially not three little kids, getting bugs from our untreated tank water. Pointing to a tap at the side of the house, I shared a sacred family secret. "Underneath where we're standing right now is a 25,000-litre water tank. The stuff that comes out of it is filtered, cleaner than rainwater. Don't tell anyone, okay?"

Jake put his water bag under the faucet and I turned it on.

"Do you understand what that means? We have something most other people don't have right now. Water. Lots of it. And it comes into the house, into this tap even, cleaned by a filtration system. We have the stuff of life. You're safe here, Jake. Safer than anywhere else you could be."

Jake smiled. Maybe a vodka smile but he looked happy. As the bags filled, I boasted a little more about the food supplies and the big propane tank that was also buried in the yard. Jake cheered up considerably and that made me feel better about everything. Then he hoisted the two heavy water sacks and tagged behind me like a beast of burden.

In front of the fence, Mr. Mueller had his arms crossed in front of him, as if he was holding himself together. Michael stood beside him. They watched other neighbours settling down for the night.

"I hope the government gets things sorted out soon," Mr. Mueller said.

"The government can't take care of each and every one of us, Harry," Michael said. "How many times has Tony said that?"

About a billion. Maybe two.

"Thanks for the water" was all Mr. Mueller said as he hefted the water bags and started toward his house. Michael went after him, took one of the bags, and the two of them disappeared around the corner of the house.

At that moment, an aftershock rocked us again. The tremors moved up my legs and made me swing side-to-side. It lasted longer than the one before. Jake and I dropped to the ground and covered our heads. More dust spewed out of the cracked earth. On the front porch a glass skittered across the table and smashed to the ground. Several neighbours shrieked. Jake's face went white.

CHAPTER 13 | RULES ARE MADE FOR BREAKING

NORTH VANCOUVER

When it ended, Jake was wild-eyed and sweating again. If Michael caught that lunatic look, he'd blame me for bringing a weak link, a drain on resources, into the compound, even if he had agreed to it. I helped Jake to his feet, and tugged him close. Then I pinched the inside of his upper arm, hard and fast.

"Ouch. Whadidya do that for?" He yanked away from me and blinked frantically.

"You need to wake up a bit, Jake." I said it kindly as I could. I was scared too and I needed to snap both of us out of it. Once I climbed on the panic train, I might never get off. "When you freak out like that, it frightens me too."

He needed a crash course in being brave. I stood and gnashed my teeth. He rubbed his arm and zipped his lips. At least he was smart enough not to say anything.

"Hey, we're all scared but we can't give into that. Fear is like a small fire—if you let it take get out of control it destroys everything in its path. We have to hang on and be brave, you know, to help each other."

"Sorry," Jake said in a wisp of voice. "I *want* to be strong. I don't know how."

"I don't know how either," I said. "But I know how to fake it."

Michael marched past us. His posture was extra rigid, and that said he was worried. More worried than he had been half an hour ago. He threw us a glance. "How're you doing, Jake?"

"Fine," Jake said and managed a half convincing smile. "I could use another drink."

Michael took the stairs two at a time. "I'd hate to see you drink alone."

"No more booze," I said.

"Did you hear something, Jake?" Michael stopped on the porch and put his hand to his ear like he was hard of hearing. "I thought I heard a fly buzzing around."

Jake smirked then caught the dark look on my face and tried to seem serious. It hardly seemed fair dragging him between the two of us, especially because Michael was a no-holds-barred fighter. I shook my head.

"Sorry, you're outnumbered." Michael laughed, picked up the bottles, and stormed into the house.

In the kitchen, I watched him pour three drinks. A stiff one for himself. A smaller one for Jake. Plain pop for me, again. Jake grabbed his and guzzled half of it.

"Weren't you going to sit up all night on sentry duty?" I said.

"Nope. Got a better plan," Michael licked his lips. "I'm going to turn the fence back on and let it do the work."

"Turn on the fence?" asked Jake with a lopsided smile.

"It's wired to give trespassers a sharp jolt." Michael refilled his glass and I pretended not to notice. "You weren't here this afternoon when some local gangbangers came around wanting a place to crash. We turned on the juice and they got the message. I turned it off once they were gone but we'll leave it on at night. That'll make any would-be burglars think twice."

"Is that legal?"

"Is it legal for you to be sitting here drinking?"

"It is in Germany," Jake said. "And I drink at home all the time."

"Yeah, I believe you." I gave Jake the stink eye.

"It's true," he protested. "Mom has a drink every night. I'm her bartender and I always mix me one too."

Michael gave me a *WTF* look and then smiled at Jake. "Well in Germany, Jake, I'm sure it's legal to have an electrified fence. How about some more *Westeros*?"

Michael had to be jittery if he was volunteering to play a board game. For me, the only thing more boring than playing that game was watching someone else play it. I left them to their pretend world, half a bottle of vodka, and a litre of orange pop.

Everything was getting out of control. I needed to see Tony. Soon. He had to know what was going on. Michael wouldn't tell Tony that he gave Javier water because Javier hadn't planned properly. I was certain that Javier wouldn't mention it either. I was the only one who would tell Tony the truth. I was going to see him no matter what they said. I would find out what he wanted us to do.

I went into Tony's room and found his gym bag, which I filled with a toothbrush, comb, pyjamas, vitamin supplements, and low-dose aspirin. I packed his favourite comfort food: chocolate-covered, dried blueberries. As a joke I put in *The Worst-Case Scenario Survival Handbook* from his bookshelf. Last of all I sat down and wrote a get-well note. I signed it with hugs and kisses and tucked it into the top of the bag. I left it by the front door and went downstairs to bed.

The warm rumble of Michael and Jake's voices in the room above me made the night feel safer, even if I was supremely pissed at Michael. Misty hopped up beside me and kneaded the edge of my pillow, purring loudly. I left the light on and stared at the ceiling. It was covered with pictures of Bolivian women wrestlers. *Lucha libre de Cholitas.* On the far wall I could see the gold medal hockey players I tried to copy: Hayley Wickenheiser, Colleen Sostorics, and Marie-Philip Poulin. On the wall over the bookshelves were pictures of some women Mom hoped I would admire: Margherita Hack, Frida Kahlo, J.K. Rowling, Germaine Greer. In between were black-and-white photos of the best girl band ever, The Savages. These were my heroes and meant-to-be-heroes. I needed to be tough, physically and mentally, like them.

I lay there and tried to make sense of what had happened in the space of a single day. I got up that morning like any other day. At that point I could talk to or text anyone in the whole world. I could lose myself in the forest for hours, away from the craziness of the world. I could take a bus across town. I could go to the beach. I could rent a movie. I could go to the mall. A few short minutes changed everything.

I had no idea what tomorrow would bring. Where would I be in a week? Would I still be locked behind a fence? Still looking at neighbours like they might steal our food or water?

It didn't feel like fourteen hours since I got out of bed, it felt like another lifetime. I had the same hands and face and legs I woke with that morning. But would anything ever be the same again? I told myself it would. It had to be. But my worried thoughts slammed into each other like shunting train cars, loud, noisy, and impossible to ignore.

After a while I heard Jake stumble into our shared bathroom. He talked to Michael in a drunken whisper. The toilet flushed. The door opened and closed. Next up Michael. He peed like a racehorse, loud and long. He drunk-whispered back to Jake. He sang as he brushed his teeth. I imagined the mirror covered in toothpaste gobs. They were gross and obnoxious, but they were my lifeline. I finally fell asleep, and dreamed I was lost in a forest, a dark forest where my screams were drowned out by the cries of people I could not see.

I woke up early, before sunrise even. A stellar jay scolded nearby. Chickadees whistled. Daybreak at camp. I smelled the roses that bloomed outside my bedroom window. As long as I lay there, I could pretend everything was okay with the world, that Mom was an easy phone call away. I dropped my hand by the side of the bed, to the spot where Oliver always slept, as if I wished hard enough then his wet nose would bump me back like it did every morning. All I got was the harsh reminder that Oliver wasn't there, that he was gone.

That reminded me that Tony would not be sitting in the kitchen, reading the paper with one hand cupped around his morning espresso. An anvil crushed my chest and I closed my eyes and waited for the pain to stop.

"Tony," I whispered. "Please be safe."

Beside me Misty stretched. She yawned a cloud of fish breath and the last scraps of normality dimmed. I stroked her and made plans. Michael wouldn't agree to me going out today. Too bad. I was going to see Tony. Period. Tony always said members of a family stay strong by looking after each other. I would stay strong by helping him. He never needed me before but I knew, as certain as I knew Saturday followed Friday, that he needed me now. I knew he'd yell at me for coming but I didn't care. I wanted him to know everything was okay. Also,

I wanted to tell him about Jake so he'd get my version of the story first.

After I fed Misty, I engaged my supersonic hearing powers but the only noise coming from Michael's room was stereo snoring. I crept upstairs like a master spy and stuffed water, sandwiches, fruit, and even a few dog things into my pack, just in case. This would be a double mission: visit Tony and look for Oliver. Maybe Oliver was somewhere in the neighbourhood, trapped behind some rubble, unable to get back to us.

I strapped the can of bear spray onto my belt. I stopped and listened again for any sounds from downstairs. Nothing. At last I tiptoed into Tony's office. The CCTV screens showed a quiet yard. The air outside was still filmy with dust from the movement of the earth and the upheaval of buildings. No one was visible on the parts of the street I could see. The control panel showed that the electricity on the fence was live. I turned it off and studied Tony's sleeping computer. His satellite broadband would still be working. Only I didn't know his password.

Once I'd tried to crack it and ended up locking down the computer. That caper got me grounded for a month. I should have known better because everything about Tony was designed to keep people out. No wonder Mom refused to move into this house with him. She said the duplex in Kitsilano was our home. This place was his, his alone. Ever since my grandparents died he'd gotten worse. He'd tried to protect himself from every possible external threat. In the end he couldn't protect himself against a random act of carelessness.

I fished under the bottom of the huge fire extinguisher beside Tony's desk and found the key to his filing cabinet. I slid open the bottom drawer, pushed aside all the files, and dug out the big zip-lock bag stashed at the back. All the keys were on separate rings and of course they were all labelled with different-coloured tags. I took one off the split ring marked "super padlock."

I had just closed the filing cabinet when the stairs from the basement creaked. Footsteps thumped into the kitchen. I stowed the bear spray under the desk with my backpack and stuck my head around the corner. Michael was staring into the fridge.

"Hey," I said.

"Hey back at you. What're you doing in the office?"

"Just checking the CCTV's. I thought I saw something by the fence but it was just a raccoon. You're up kind of early, aren't you?"

"I need something to feed my hangover."

"Raw eggs?"

He frowned and pulled out two plastic containers. "Steak and potatoes should do."

I went out to the front porch, picked up the binoculars, and acted like I was on sentry duty. It felt like hours before Michael's dishes clattered into the sink and I waited for the sound of him going down to the basement. The next thing I knew he was standing behind me. "See anything?"

"Not much. Thought I'd just sit and see what happens next."

"What happens next is I go back to bed."

I watched him go down the hall, glancing into Tony's office as he went. I coughed loudly and he looked back at me. Good. He didn't see my backpack. I forced myself to wait another ten minutes. Standing on the front porch, I checked out the fence line for any threatening people. When I was satisfied that no one was hanging around to ambush me, I slipped out the gate with Tony's gym bag. Phase one of the plan completed. Some people stirred in their front yards so I walked faster. I didn't want to be within hailing distance if Michael heard me leave. I revved my pace to a speed walk, determined to be halfway to the hospital before he discovered I was gone.

"Freedom." I punched the air as I turned the corner onto Swanston Road. Then I stopped as my gut scrambled. The aftershocks had hit this area hard. On my street all the houses were new, built in the last few years to stricter seismic standards. They stood pretty straight and tall still. People could probably go back inside but most chose not to.

Here the houses, what had been houses yesterday, were ancient. Today they were crushed heaps waiting for a bulldozer. Tony joked they were built before electricity was invented and predicted that they couldn't stand up to an earthquake but I didn't believe him. He always saw the entire world through a haze of disaster gloom. Who would have guessed his spooky predictions would come true?

CHAPTER 14 | MEAN STREETS

NORTH VANCOUVER

Some yards had tents. One family sat around a table outside their RV. The wheels of it were wedged in a crevice in the road. The crooked house that had the Kawasaki for sale last month looked deserted. There was no sign of the motorbike anywhere. I passed a cedar hedge that had been wrenched in half by a rupture in the ground. In the middle of the pervasive odour of smoke, the torn branches smelled like Mom's house at Christmas.

That simple smell transported me to last December. I lay in front of the fire with Oliver curled behind my knees. The soles of my feet were getting really hot but I didn't want to move because Oliver was sleeping so peacefully. Mom was sitting cross-legged on the sofa with a spool of red satin ribbon in her lap. She was making bows to tie around railings on the front porch. Outside the first snow of winter sifted down from a leaden sky. Mom and I were talking about Christmas dinner and what we needed to make the day before and what everyone else was bringing. The back door slammed and we heard Michael's boots hit the kitchen floor. When he walked into the living room he was almost hidden behind an armful of cedar branches. The sweet smell of cedar rushed ahead of him and filled the room.

It hurt to remember that, to think how different everything was now. That world of simple holiday fun seemed on the other side of a dark, bottomless river. If this was a movie, dramatic music would be playing in the background. Only I couldn't hear even a car on the quiet streets. Silence made the scene of twisted houses and cracked roads more vivid. When I reached the main drag I hoped to see buses chugging along even though I couldn't hear any. It was empty except for one police car in the middle of the intersection at Mountain Highway. Portable traffic barricades squatted in front of the Mountie cruiser to stop people from turning onto Lynn Valley Road. A guy on a bicycle was arguing with the Mounties beside the barricade.

"Hey man, it's just a bike," the cyclist said.

"Doesn't matter. Lynn Valley Road is closed to everything but emergency response vehicles," the woman officer said.

"I haven't seen many of those around, have you?"

"Do you want us to book you right now, or would you like to be on your way?" The male officer lifted his hat and mopped his forehead with the back of his hand. His face glowed red. "What're you looking at?" he growled at me.

"Nothing," I said and backed away.

"Hey," the woman called me.

"Yes?" I stopped and widened my face in an innocent expression. I was innocent but just being spoken to by a cop made me nervous. I squared my shoulders and drew myself up to my full height of five feet, ten inches.

"You got a place to go?" She pierced me with her eyes, waiting for my answer.

"Yeah, yeah. I do."

"Well make sure you go there because there's a twenty-four hour curfew starting at noon. Only essential travel will be allowed." She tucked her thumbs into her belt and shifted most of her weight to her back left leg, like a martial artist in a high stance.

I glanced at my watch. 8:00. I had four hours. The hospital was only half an hour away if I walked slowly. I could be there and home again before curfew started.

I broke into a jog. I didn't expect her to chase me but I wanted to put as much distance between us as I could.

I checked over my shoulder one last time. Would the cop have helped me if she knew Tony was an ex-Mountie? I didn't think so. Tony said the young officers had no respect for old guys like him.

Old guys like him.

He wasn't so old. He was my father and we needed him at home.

I picked my way along an alternate route to the hospital. As I walked, I searched for Oliver behind every tree, in every yard. I didn't see many other people on the way but when I got to Grand Boulevard I found the huge park had been turned into an emergency campground. Hundreds of people swarmed around tents of every size and shape. Some were just tarpaulins on wires attached to rough posts. Was everyone really homeless or had they left their homes and sticking together for safety? I crossed to the west side of the refugee camp and didn't make eye contact with anyone.

The coolness of night had disappeared and sun baked the earth again. My hair, wet and woolly, clung to my neck. It was like when I went on a big hike. I'd get halfway up the trail and feel tired and frustrated. Then I'd wish I could turn around. But reaching the summit was always worth it so I forged on. When I saw Tony it'd be worth it. More than.

On the hill above the soccer fields at 15th, I stopped to gaze down at yet another camping ground. The tennis courts at the far end of the field held a dozen or so dogs. They barked and danced around the feet of a woman who held a large bag of dry food. I squinted but I didn't see one that looked like Oliver. As I started to edge down the grassy slope toward them, I skimmed the city horizon and froze in my tracks.

Half the downtown skyscrapers had disappeared. Even at this distance I could see the rubble where office towers and apartment buildings once stood. A man, lying on the hill with a towel for a pillow said, "No one ever thought it'd be this bad, eh?"

I shook my head and sank into a crouch. *Slow deep breaths. Stop. Think. Observe. Plan.* Could I plan my way out of this disaster? Of course not but I had to survive it, to wait for the world to pull itself together and rebuild.

"May as well pull up a piece of grass," the man said and yanked his dusty baseball cap down over his eyes. "This is as good a place as any to park yourself. At least if you're out in the open, you're not going to get crushed under a house or a tree."

I tensed my body to lock out the alarm that threatened to turn my bones to water. All thoughts of Oliver flew from my mind. I stood, shook the stiffness out of my legs, and started to run. I had to see Tony.

I ran past busted cars and broken houses. I let the sound of my footfalls lull me out of my anxiety. Left right, left right. Keep thinking about seeing Tony, nothing more.

Just before I got to the hospital, I had to detour around a massive sinkhole. I arrived drenched in sweat and panting hard. A small crowd milled outside temporary barricades. Inside the bright orange barriers, a dozen cops clustered under the shade of purple-leafed cherry trees. They all wore Kevlar vests and had batons tucked in their belts. Their eyes tracked the mob the way border collies watch sheep. One cop held his hand over his pistol and I wondered if there had been trouble or if he was only anticipating some. A handwritten sign was stuck on a sandwich board: *medical personnel, hospital staff and new (seriously injured and sick) patients and ONE carer only past this point. No visitors. No journalists. No exceptions. Line up here to see a triage nurse.*

I fell into the line to see the two nurses who sat at a folding table under a big umbrella. A cop stood beside them, stony-faced behind sunglasses. In front of me, a tall skinny kid wore brand-new runners caked with blood from a deep cut on his shin. He leaned on his mother who was an older version of him in her tank top, faded cut-offs, and the same curly blond hair. There were three groups of people in front of them, which was a pretty short line up. I'd get in to see Tony after all.

The woman in front of me stomped her feet and sighed impatiently. Behind me a man with an injured wrist moaned and swore. I braced myself against their infectious hostility and gloom. To distance myself from them, I pulled out my phone and flipped through my pictures. I had hundreds but not a single one of Tony. Mostly I had shots of me, Lexy, and Oliver. When the boy in front of me got to the nurse, she checked his wound and shot a few quick words at the other nurse. They handed him a package of bandages and Betadine swipes and told him to keep it clean. As he and his mother walked away grumbling, I realized not a single person in the line up had been taken into the hospital, not even the tiny old lady who was carried by two young boys.

"Symptoms?" the nurse snapped at me and scribbled something on a piece of paper.

"I want to see my father."

"Next," she called to the man behind me who pushed me aside. He shoved a swollen wrist at her. His hand hung limp, as if he had no bones in his arm.

"Excuse me," I said to the young Mountie behind the nurses. She might be easier to persuade than the triage staff.

She raised her chin. "Yeah?"

"I need to see my father."

"He's already in the hospital?"

"Yeah he came in yesterday."

"So who brought him here?"

"Uncle Javier." I said slowly, understanding where this was going.

"That's his one carer then, isn't it?"

"Yes but he doesn't have any of his things with him. He needs clean clothes and his razor. He's an ex-Mountie and is very particular about his personal grooming."

She knotted her mouth and then held out her hand. I pushed the bag at her and she opened it and checked the insides. Desperation clawed at me and I tried not to recoil at the smell of BO that clung to her. She had to be cooking in that uniform. I pointed to the luggage tag with his name and cell number on it. She closed the bag with a terse nod of her head.

"Can you tell me anything about him?" I begged, holding back panic with every ounce of willpower I had.

She frowned and it seemed that she was trying to decide if I was worth the bother.

"Please." I tried to keep the whine out of my voice.

"I'll see what I can find out." She sauntered back to the group under the cherry trees and talked into a crackly walkie-talkie for a few minutes. Then she walked toward me, her face expressionless.

"Your father has a gun?" At that last word, the man with the fractured wrist looked at me sharply. I felt his antenna twitch.

"Yes, but he has a licence."

"I hope it's properly stored." Her tone cut like a knife.

"It is. It is. After the accident we locked it away. It's in a hidden safe." I whispered because the man was staring now.

The Mountie paused for a minute and then she touched my arm. Her pale white hand, with its plain gold wedding band and square fingertips, felt cool on my skin. I willed her to give me only good news. But that's not what she had to offer. "Unfortunately there has been a complication. Seems your father has developed wound botulism and he'll be in the hospital for a few more days."

"Botulism? Doesn't botulism come from rotten food?" My voice came out high and squeaky.

"It's airborne and gets into open wounds too. With all the dirt and ground stirred up right now, well, anything's possible."

"But—"

She held up her hand like she was stopping traffic. "But nothing. He's one of the lucky ones—he's got a bed and someone taking care of him. Now you need to take care of yourself so you can help him when he gets out. And you need to get home. A state of emergency was declared last night. As of noon today, there is a strict curfew being enforced."

"How long for?"

"Until you hear otherwise. Do you have a radio?"

My words fell into a heap so I just nodded.

"Then go home, turn it on and listen. I'll make sure your father gets his bag but don't expect to be visiting him. Not this week anyway. Phone service should be restored soon, and you can call him then."

I stumbled away from the hospital and wandered up St. Andrews Avenue, deaf and blind to everything around me. My mission had failed. Now I had to tell Michael I'd left the compound and not even seen Tony. I started to walk, to try to figure out what to do next.

CHAPTER 15 | BACK TO THE FOREST

NORTH VANCOUVER

Barely nine o'clock and already my armpits were soaked. Two days ago, the people on these side streets, the ones sitting around their front lawns, would have been on their way to work or the gym or to daycare. Instead they hovered in hushed conversations over card and camping tables.

I walked past a collapsed house where two men in overalls, with the word "Volunteer" emblazoned across the back, dug at the rubble with a crowbar. A woman in a thin sundress, clutching a teddy bear, stood beside them. The volunteers dragged part of a crib out of the wreckage. The woman wailed and fell to her knees. "No! No! No!" she screamed and pounded the toy with her fist.

As I passed, the volunteers glanced at me with lifeless eyes. I saw a stroller crushed under the flattened front stairs and shivered. For the first time in my life, I understood what the word *surreal* meant.

Only twenty-four hours ago, the people who lived here were having everyday arguments and worries. They laughed at silly jokes, planned holidays and argued over back-to-school supplies. Where were they when the quake hit? At work in an office tower? Buying eggs at the supermarket? Swimming in the sea? What did they think about in that minute that changed the world so drastically?

That made me think about Mom again. Be safe, Mom, wherever you are. She might be dead. That pierced my heart. No, I prayed. Not that. Busy. Stay busy. Think about something else.

Okay: yesterday morning. A bowl of blackberries and three slices of toast for breakfast. Two for me. One for Oliver. I was thinking about school starting and Lexy coming home. This year her parents promised her a credit card to do all her own shopping. She'd been emailing me about what she wanted to buy and I was going with her. I'd take some of my babysitting and cat feeding money and buy new runners. That was yesterday. How long before our lives would be back to normal?

The woman stopped howling and hugged the teddy bear. Her gaze followed me and she seemed sad and angry all at once, as if I had no right to be alive and breathing while her baby was buried or worse. I bent my head and walked faster.

I needed somewhere quiet and alone to think. I had to get away from Michael, who seemed to have forgotten Tony's basic rules. I needed to get away from Jake and his demands for reassurance. I needed private space to think my own thoughts before they were drowned by someone else's.

Numbly, I wound my way down the back lanes and hidden pathways, over the cracks in the pavement, all the way back to the forest. Aftershocks had opened more gullies and brought down more big branches. The forest looked fiercely unfriendly. I called, "Oliver," loudly. A couple of fallen trees made a large X, like a hostile *Keep Out* sign. I thought of the first explorers who came to this canyon when the trees were centuries old. The thick evergreens would have been as dark as a cave. But still the explorers pressed on. Now it was quiet and empty and I pushed myself into its silent embrace.

The canopy had opened and sun shone brighter on the forest floor than it had since logging had stopped, a hundred years ago. It illuminated the thick layer of dust that covered everything. I hiked in with only the crunch of my own footsteps for company. Losing all track of time and place, I climbed higher and higher as if I could escape all the misery below the mountain, as if the mangled forest was no more than a movie set. When my hands started to shake around noon, I sat down and tried to eat.

As I bit into an apple, the shrill scream of a red-tailed hawk sent goosebumps down my arms. I jumped to my feet and tramped toward the trail where I'd last seen Oliver. Not a sign of him. I clambered through the vacant park, and for the next hour checked under fallen timber and around gullies and landslips. I called his name and strained my ears to hear a yap or a whine in reply. An occasional crow or jay squawked. I didn't see another person. A helicopter sawed through the distant sky. I scrambled over the smashed trees and picked my way around twisted ground. I tried to forget the raccoon crushed by a boulder, a bald eagle feasting on a rat, and a coyote running away with a long, fleshy bone in its mouth.

As the sun crested in the sky, I trudged on. Blackberry bushes scraped my legs. With my throat raw from calling, I sat again and listened for a single hint that Oliver was there. The heavy silence made my ears ache. It was as if the end of the world had come and no one had bothered to tell me. I stood, desperate for someone to talk to. Someone who wasn't Michael and wasn't Jake.

I went back to the suburbs, to the chaos there. I wandered neighbourhood streets calling Oliver's name half-heartedly, telling myself not to think about Mom or Tony. Everywhere I turned it looked like places had been bombed. How many times had I heard people say this place or that place looked like a war zone? But this *did* look like a war zone. Only a nuclear war could have made things look worse. I wanted to take pictures of the burnt houses to show Michael how bad it was. But I didn't. It seemed sick to record other people's misery. I stowed my phone and kept walking and calling.

By the time I reached Wakeford Drive I hadn't seen a single person walking around, only me. I guess most people had heard about the curfew. Guilty nervousness made my hands sweat and I wiped them on my jeans. If I got busted for breaking curfew, I'd be grounded for life. I hurried down the hill toward the Skodas. Seeing the twins that I babysat every Monday would cheer me up. I had a chocolate bar they could have and I'd love to hear Mrs. Skoda's happy laugh.

I'd never noticed before how so many of the houses on this street were old, very old. Most were badly damaged and no one stirred around any of the collapsed buildings. The Skoda house, at the bottom of the hill, was the best of a bad lot. It leaned sideways, as if someone had given it a big shove, but at least it still looked like a house.

A pipe had ruptured somewhere close and the stench of raw sewage poisoned the air. Again the end-of-the-earth feeling skittered through my chest. From behind the Skodas' place, a murmur of voices reached me. As I walked closer, something told me to stay back. I cupped my hands around my mouth. "Hello? Is anyone home?"

Laughter rumbled from the back yard and a guy came through the side gate. At the sight of him a scorching ball of panic flared up my throat. His toque confirmed the worst; the fluorescent green skull on a black background was the official logo of the Green Death gang.

"Whaddaya want?" he sneered.

I wanted to turn and run but instead I forced out, "Are the Skodas here?"

"Who're they?" He folded his arms and his spider tattoos flexed and doubled in size.

"They live here." Every lick of moisture in my mouth evaporated.

"Why don't you come around back and check," Green Toque said. His lech look made me feel naked in five different ways. I glanced toward the side gate. What other gang members were back there? What was the last thing Red said to me? *You're going to wish you was dead.*

"Never mind. If you see them please say that Lexy called?" *Sorry, BF.*

"And what did your last fucken slave die of?" He laughed and made a production of horking a big gob on the lawn. He pushed his toque up slightly as if he was inspecting a piece of meat.

My heart tried to pound its way out of my ribcage and I inched away. Green Toque moved forward and grabbed my arm. His hands were rough and callused and his chewed nails were black. "Where're ya going? What're ya afraid of?"

Stop. Think. Don't let him smell your fear. Small green dots of terror rose at the corners of my eyes. I forced a smile. "My brother's waiting around the corner. He said he'd give me five minutes to check on the Skodas." I made a show of turning my wrist to see my watch. My hand shook and I tightened it into a fist. "Time's up. I'd better go."

"You're right. Your time *is* up." Red rounded the corner with two more thugs in tow. "She's that bitch from the crazy guy's house. She's the one that burned me on the fence." He held up his slightly pink palms. What a wimp. My hands were ten times worse after a good hockey game. He took three fast steps and got so close that I smelled his cigarette stink. He bared his teeth. "She's mine."

I jerked my arm away and stumbled as I stepped off the curb. Like wolves stalking prey, the four of them fanned out and moved forward. Red leered and reached a hand toward my crotch and I opened my mouth and screamed long and loud. They stopped, stunned, just long enough for me to slip the canister out of the pouch on my belt. In a single fluid motion I swept the pepper can in front of me.

"Fuck off!" I said. I'd never used the f-word before, and it felt strong and satisfying, as if I'd crossed a line into toughness and invincibility. My index finger found the trigger. The guys slithered closer.

"Stay back," My voice warbled.

"Three, two, one..." Red lunged at me at the same time as his buddies. I sprayed a cloud in a semicircle over them. They shrieked and covered their faces.

"You're dead," Red yelled. "You and your brother're both dead."

"Get some water," one of them shouted and they staggered toward the back yard, clutching their faces and holding onto each other for support. I raced away, faster than I'd ever run in my life. At the end of the street I checked over my shoulder to make sure I was safe and almost ran into the path of a blue hybrid. It screeched to a halt and relief poured over me.

"Greg!" I jumped into the passenger seat and gulped for air. "I'm sure glad to see you."

"I heard a scream and came to see who was in trouble. Was that you? Man you've got some lung power. What're you doing out here? Haven't you heard about the curfew?" The central locking of the car clicked shut and he made a jerky three-point turn. He wore the same green T-shirt as the day before but now it was wrinkled and dirty. The dreadlocks poking out from under the orange cap were unravelling and he had a thick five o'clock shadow. Me? What the hell was he doing here? "I wanted to see if the kids I babysat were okay." My excuse flopped out, a little bit of true and a lot of false.

"I thought you were going to take care of Jake. He seems a quiet type and he sure was upset yesterday. Where's he now?" Was he kidding? What about me? Didn't he say that he heard my scream? Couldn't he tell I'd just been through something terrible? Shouldn't he be taking my pulse or giving me a hoodie or something? I could have PTSD. Where did he come from anyway and how spooky was it that he was haunting our neighbourhood?

I thought about Michael's suspicions and wondered if I'd jumped out of the proverbial frying pan. Not wanting Greg to sense my worry, I sat back and tried to appear bored. I hoped he didn't notice the way my legs trembled and my feet bounced a little jig of their own.

Besides how did he know what type of a kid Jake was? Did paramedic training give him special powers? I gulped some water from my bottle so my tongue would work. "He's at our house, my dad's place. It's like a fortress with a chain-link fence around it and totally earthquake proof. We've got tons of food and water. He couldn't be in a safer place."

"If you do have a lot of food and water, I wouldn't be telling many people about it. Those are scarce resources."

"God, I wouldn't have said anything to just anyone." I invented an answer I hoped he would believe. "And you're part of emergency services. It might be important for you to know where there's safe shelter."

He nodded with a slight smile.

"Thanks for picking me up," I said. "I can walk home from here."

"I don't think so. These streets aren't safe."

I couldn't argue with that. "Okay. Well thanks. My house is that way." I pointed, and wondered how well he knew this neighbourhood. Did he remember that Michael said we lived on Parni? I felt guilty for Michael's lie.

"You're lucky I picked you up. I saw a police car drive down this road just a few minutes ago. As long as you're with me, I can get you home with my ID."

Now who was lying? I'd been walking around for hours and I'd only seen two police cars. One on Lynn Valley Road and another at the hospital. "Our place is over there." I pointed to the end of the cul-de-sac.

"That's not Parni Place is it?"

"Michael was just being careful when he said we lived there."

"Figured he was trying to misdirect me. Especially when I saw you at Jake's place. I have to say I didn't expect a smart girl like you to need rescuing."

Yesterday he told Jake I was a woman who could take care of things. Today he called me a girl again. What a hypocrite.

"I didn't need rescuing. I was fine by myself." I said as he signalled to turn. "Please stop. I'd better walk from here."

"Your father wouldn't like seeing you brought home by a strange man, would he?" Greg pulled to the curb and unlocked the car doors. I fumbled with my seat belt.

"Tony's not home right now, but Michael is, and he's almost as paranoid as the old man. He might get the wrong idea if he saw me getting out of your car."

"Or he might get the right idea," Greg said. "He might get the idea that I'm looking out for you kids."

CHAPTER 16 | UNDER THE RUBBLE

VANCOUVER, WEST END

Twenty-four hours after the earthquake struck, Dixie Morgan lay pinned to the concrete floor under the pancaked building. Poisonous hairy spiders, as big as saucers, had punctured her nightmares. She had watched her body decay and turn into dust. Then sunshine burst through the darkness. She sat on the beach as Rowan and Michael, toddlers again, played in the sand. She reached out to touch them but they vanished as she woke to torment that wouldn't stop.

How long have I been here?

Blackness and pain had been her only companions for so long she had lost all sense of time. She had finished the small water bottle from the pocket of her cycling top ages ago. Her stomach rumbled and dryness cemented her mouth shut. *Is this hell? How long will I lie here in unrelenting pain and crippling loneliness? Am I going to die? Does anyone know where I am? Who will tell Rowan and Michael what happened to me? Will they ever know?*

Another tremor shook the earth and the building above her shifted and moaned. A fresh layer of dust sifted over her. Her throat tightened and she braced herself for death. *I love you my babies. Please forgive me.*

When the noise stopped, she heard voices nearby. People spoke excitedly. A dog barked, once.

"We've got something over here," a man called. He sounded close.

Dixie tried to call out but her voice was little more than a croak. Her mouth tasted sour. She forced herself up on her elbows and with one hand fished in the pocket of her cycling top. She opened her cell phone. As it came to life, a pale blue light illuminated her prison. *I'm not blind.* Relief flooded over her and her heart raced. *All this time I've had this thin sliver between me and insanity. I'm a fool for not thinking of it sooner.*

No service it read but she didn't care. *Thursday 4:18 PM.* That simple knowledge eased her fear. *I've been here for more than a day. Now help has arrived. I'm not going to die.* A chortling sound rose in her throat. Laughter. Twisting her hand over her shoulder, she connected with the girder and tapped the phone against the exposed steel support. *What was the code for SOS?* Three short, three long, three short. *What does a long tap sound like?* She wasn't sure so she tapped and held it on the three middle strikes.

"Hello," the male voice called. "Can you hear me?"

Dixie tried to answer but only a puff of air broke from her mouth. She tapped as fast as she could.

"Tap twice for yes."

Dixie tapped twice.

"Stay as still as you can," the man said. "We're coming."

Two fat tears pressed out of Dixie's eyes. She didn't think she had enough moisture in her body left to cry but the thought of seeing her family and friends again, the thought of not dying here, overwhelmed her. She lay her head down and waited.

CHAPTER 17 | LIFE INSIDE

NORTH VANCOUVER

"Where the hell've you been?" Michael called as I walked up the cul-de-sac. My legs shook as the last of adrenaline worked its way out of my body. I'd never been so happy to see that ten-foot fence.

The neighbours stopped talking and started acting oh-so-casual. I imagined them sharpening their ears. I pretended not to hear Michael until I neared the gate. "I went to visit Tony. Didn't you get my note?"

"How'd you get out?"

"You didn't close the lock last night so I figured you left it open for me."

"You're full of crap." The gate whined as he opened it. Jake stayed on the porch, the non-combat zone. Michael limped toward me. "You are so out of line. You thought it was okay to leave the fence turned off and me asleep? I don't believe that for one second."

I refused to argue or apologize. "What happened to your leg?"

He hobbled up the stairs and turned around at the front door. His words blazed. "The Redgraves tried to get in this morning. If Don Redgrave wasn't such a loudmouth we might have ended up with him, his wife, and their jackass boys living with us." Michael sighed long and heavy: a windup for the guilt trip he was about to lay on me. "Anyway I charged up the stairs from the basement so fast I missed the top step and twisted my ankle."

"You should have heard him swear," Jake said, grinning. Michael and I glared at him and he sat back and studied his fingernails.

I followed Michael inside, hoping to keep his lecture to me as private as possible.

"I got the electricity back on though. Apparently some of the neighbours saw you saunter away. Harry Mueller said everyone was talking about the way you just let yourself out of here and the Redgraves figured that the fence must be turned off." When Michael frowned, he became Tony's twin. "You put us all at risk, Rowan. Way uncool. Don't you get it? We have to protect this place until Tony's back. And in case you haven't heard, there's an effing curfew and you could've been busted. And what would Tony say to that?"

I didn't ask how he would explain being so hungover he didn't even hear me leave the house. I slid that ace up my sleeve. "Don't worry about it. I think the curfew's only theoretical. I've seen exactly two cop cars out there and way more homeless people than you could imagine." I rubbed my arm. It still throbbed from where Green Toque had grabbed me, not that I'd breathe a word of that to Michael.

"Anyway the power was off to let you in but it's going back on again." He stepped into the office and flicked the switch.

"From now on, we're sticking to a serious eight-hour watch each. We've got no idea how long we're going to be here."

He went into the kitchen and I followed. My body felt as dry as a sea monkey and I sucked back three glasses of water. He flopped down at the table and picked up his PSP.

"So how is Tony?" he said.

"I didn't get to see him."

Michael pounded his fist on the table. "Then where the hell have you been?"

"Walking. Thinking. Trying to find Oliver."

"You're so self-centred! Searching for your dog when we have this whole house to look after."

"D'you want to know what I found out about Tony?"

He nodded and shut up for half a second. When he was mad he turned into a one-way valve, only capable of dishing out words, not taking any in. So I talked fast while I had his limited attention. I jumped right in with the bit at the hospital and how the Mountie took Tony's bag and then got on the walkie-talkie to get more information about him.

"Wound botulism? Is that even possible?" Michael squinted.

"That's what I said. The cop said it's airborne."

"Could we catch it off him?" Jake interrupted from behind me.

"Good one, Jake," I said. "Just think about yourself."

"At least he was here to help me."

"We listened to the radio." Jake sat across the table from Michael and stared out the window.

Michael opened his outflow valve. "What we heard was worse than ever. There's still no power, no internet, only satellite signals city-wide and beyond. A huge tsunami hit Vancouver Island. Some neighbourhoods in Richmond have been being sucked into liquefaction fields. There're hundreds of thousands of people missing. No one knows how many people are buried in buildings all over the place. And it's not just Vancouver; the quake rocked the coast from California to Alaska. Four major cities have been hit: Victoria, Vancouver,

Seattle, and Portland. And all the little cities and towns in between." Michael pushed his hands through his hair and bent his head. When he looked up, sparks flew from his eyes. "You better shape up. We don't just have to be smart now. We have to be uber-smart."

"God, is that your plan? We're going to lock ourselves in here forever?"

"If we have to. Tony said what we're supposed to stay inside and don't let anyone in. That's exactly what we're going to do."

A wintry chill crawled down my arms at the thought of being stuck in the compound forever. Okay not forever but it sure would only feel like forever. I hugged myself, as if I could banish all the horrors of the past day and the bleak future ahead. *Please let mom be okay. Please let Tony get well soon.*

Jake snapped his gum and folded a napkin into a fan shape. He handed it to me, a hopeful smile lifting his face. I smiled back as I accepted it but my voice quavered with guilt when I said to Michael "Is your ankle okay?"

"Of course." He slammed his chair back under the table. "Spare me your sympathy. I'm going back to bed. I'm taking the graveyard shift every night, Jake gets three to eleven because he asked for it and he was here. That means you get 7 AM to 3 PM, being as you like to get up so early."

Without another word he lumbered downstairs. I turned back to Jake. "What a hothead. As if I can't take care of myself."

"He was pretty worried about you." Jake rubbed his nose. "So was I."

"Did you get lunch?" It was almost dinnertime but I needed to change the subject.

"Yep. Two peanut butter and banana sandwiches."

I sighed at the hopelessness that was Jake. "I hope you enjoyed those, Jake. These bananas are all we have, probably for a very long time. If the whole of the West Coast has been hit, it may be a while before there are any more bananas in Vancouver. You might want to learn to eat a little differently." My voice didn't sound guilty or frightened at all now. It sounded aggressive and mean. Like Tony.

For what was left of the afternoon, Jake and I worked in the garden. Of course he'd never worked in the dirt before—his parents had a la-di-dah service that cut their lawn and weeded their flowerbeds. Jake thought gardening was a treat and refused to wear gloves, said he liked the earth under his fingernails. He weeded two garden beds in the time it took me to do one. At one point aftershocks shuddered the ground beneath our feet, and I dragged him down beside me. We held hands tight and he looked at me with wild eyes. I said in an exaggerated casual voice, "This is all sooooo boring, isn't it?"

His Adam's apple bobbed when he swallowed. When the aftershocks stopped and we dusted ourselves off, he asked, "Where d'you think my mom is?"

"Your mom?" I faked a smile. "She's downtown, ordering everyone around, telling the troops to get those damn bridges fixed so she can get back here and resume command as the Grand Empress of the North Shore." He laughed, a deep rich sound. I got to my feet and handed him a hose. "Okay each plant gets a quick drink. Count to five slowly, then water the next one."

He watered with his left hand and, with his right, popped a cherry tomato into his mouth. "Mm. My favourite," he said, still chewing. Then, self-consciously, "Mom's the reason I'm vegetarian."

"Really."

"Yeah I'm vegetarian because she is. But sometimes when just my dad and I go out, we eat chicken and don't tell her."

"I won't tell her if you want to eat meat with us."

"Thanks. And I'm sorry if your dad finds me, and you get into trouble. I know he'll probably kick me out." His tone was quiet and wistful.

If he were on the outside alone, left to forage in the crowds I'd seen today, he wouldn't have a clue how to survive. If he was going to survive inside, he needed a speed lesson in how to deal with Tony. I said, "I'm going to tell you something that you can't tell anyone else, okay?"

He nodded.

"I know it's hard to talk to people sometimes," I said. I crushed a tomato leaf between my forefinger and thumb and sniffed its summery scent. I was marooned with Jake; we might as well be friends. "When I was ten I looked pretty androgynous." I laughed a bit at the memory. "I didn't even know what that word meant back then."

He showered the tomato plant with water.

"All I knew was that I liked it when no one was sure if I was a boy or a girl. I kept my hair really, really short. I only wore jeans and hoodies and high-top runners." I hadn't spoken about this for so long the words felt alien in my mouth, as if I were telling a dark fairytale. I watched the water pool around the bottom of one tomato plant, then another. The wet earth smell floated up from the garden bed. The sun warmed my skin and a thrush sang a spiralling call in the trees behind the house. Fortress Tony was a good place to tell secrets and feel safe.

"I was tall back then too. I've always been in the upper percentile for height." Jake nodded again and I spoke slowly. "One day I got to the rink and there were a bunch of older boys—grade six or seven—playing pickup hockey. They'd already started and one team was way better than the other. The captain of the good team said 'you look like a loser. You can play with them.' He didn't know that I was playing in the girls' gold league." I pulled a few weeds and took a big breath. "That made me mad so I showed off. I scored on them lots and we won six-zero. My team invited me to come back and play the next day. I said I couldn't because I was playing for the championship. You should have seen their faces when they realized that the only championship game that day was the girls' division."

I smiled at the memory of how good that moment felt, letting those obnoxious boys know they had been beaten by a girl. Jake smiled back at me as if he was waiting for the happy ending to the story. I shook my head. For all that I wanted to hang on to that one golden moment, I couldn't. "The leader of the other team called me a bitch. I just said, 'thanks for the practice' and walked away. The losing team came after me. At the far end of the park they dragged me inside the boys' washroom, twisted my arms behind my back and shoved my face into a toilet again and again."

Jake gaped at me.

"I thought I was going to drown. I don't know how long I was in there. It felt like they kept me prisoner forever. Then a dog walker came along with his two big labs. He heard me crying and stormed into the washroom. His dogs went apeshit at all the excitement. The boys ran away."

"The thing is, I didn't speak to hardly anyone for the next year or so. I didn't want to, but mostly I just couldn't. Even when I did want to talk, the words just wouldn't come." I dug the muddy toe of my runner into the earth and remembered the long silent months when the only person I could speak to was Mom.

She was the one who suggested I get a dog. Before that, I'd begged and begged for one and she'd refused to have any pets at all. After the incident in the park, as she called it, she said I needed a safe friendship and a new responsibility, someone to take my mind off myself.

"Mom was good and gentle about it but Tony lost his sympathy really fast. After about a month he tried to push me into talking, like I wanted to be silent, like I wasn't still paralyzed by shock."

I didn't tell Jake all this to make him feel sorry for me. I wanted him to understand Tony better. "What I'm saying is, Tony doesn't like silence. If I go quiet he hassles me. He says stuff like, 'If you don't speak for yourself, who's going to speak up for you? No one respects a person who can't stand up for herself.'"

Jake looked at me, clearly not getting my message. "Jake, I'm telling you this so that if Tony finds you here, you don't freeze again. You have to tell him you need to stay here. Tell him your house is a wreck. And don't let him know that you're afraid. Michael and I will defend you but Tony will listen more if you speak for yourself. Way more than if you shut down."

Jake nodded and moved to the next row of vegetables, to the herbs and kale. I followed. "Really, I know that it can be hard to talk to people. Sometimes you feel like you just can't." I picked a snail off a head of lettuce and lobbed it toward the compost heap. "Sometimes, when I get mad or impatient with you, it's because you are so quiet. Sometimes you remind me of my silent months."

"Thanks for explaining," Jake said. He spoke as he always did, by barely opening his mouth. He dropped his chin so his hair shielded his face. "I was bullied when I went to school in Dubai. That's why I get homeschooled."

He didn't offer any more details and I didn't ask. We both knew something had changed between us. But what about when Tony came home?

Lost in thought, I didn't see Don Redgrave walk up to the fence but I heard him when he started to shout, "You hoarding bastards. Tell your father that he's going to get his. The rest of us are dying of thirst out here and you're watering your garden." He scowled at us for a few minutes before stomping away.

"Wow. He's scarier than the earthquake was." I spoke calmly but I had to rub the chill out of my arms. Jake flicked the hair off his face and smiled. Strangely it felt like he was comforting me.

I wondered where Michael was. Ordinarily he was a light sleeper and Don Redgrave hadn't exactly been whispering. He was probably just tired from his injury. I turned my thoughts back to Jake and rushed to keep things business-as-usual. "Mr. Redgrave doesn't know this is grey water. It comes from the showers and sinks. It's been filtered once but it wouldn't be safe to drink even if we gave it to him. If he gets really angry, we'll tell him. But for now we don't offer any information to anyone, okay?" Water splashed around a green bean plant. "That's too much. Count faster. There, that's plenty."

I put my hand over Jake's and let a soft silence lap over us. For that moment there was only the two of us doing a job that we could see, smell, and feel. The whole world was inside-out but we had one small patch we could keep alive.

CHAPTER 18 | SMALL SPACES

VANCOUVER, WEST END

As Dixie clutched the rescue worker's hand, a voice hailed from behind him.

"Dixie? Dixie Morgan?" a woman called.

The rescue worker squeezed Dixie's hand one last time. "The pros have arrived," he said and brushed her cheek, a final gesture of kindness.

"Thanks for staying with me." Dixie closed her eyes and a coughing fit seized her. Then a pair of warm, certain hands touched hers.

"Hi Dixie, my name is Harminder Singh," the woman said. "I'm an orthopaedic surgeon. Do you know why I'm here? Did the other doctor explain your options?"

Dixie nodded as Dr. Singh took her pulse. The other doctor had explained that he was only a GP. Dixie needed a specialist, if they could get one, and a small person at that, because the cavity where Dixie lay was tiny.

"Lose my leg or kiss my butt goodbye." Dixie smiled through her tears.

Dr. Singh stroked her face. "Dr. Harrison is with me and has brought some anaesthetic but we can't give you a general. I have to warn you that this is going to be very painful." The doctor bit her lip. "I've never done a field amputation before but I'm told I'm a damned good surgeon. I'll work as fast as I can."

"I guess we're even then." Dixie's voice trilled with dread. "I've never had a field amputation before. I guess this is going to make us blood sisters or something. Let's get this show on the road."

NORTH VANCOUVER

"If you're not here when I get up, I'll change the padlock."
Michael said the next morning when I reported for my watch.
On the railing in front of him were a dozen plastic water bottles,
each one was half full of clear liquid and had a toilet paper wick
poking out. Homemade fire extinguishers. He'd made a bunch
once for a school science project and scattered around his feet
were components I recognized from that venture: a watering can,
a mega bottle of vinegar, dish soap, toilet paper and baking soda.

"In case you haven't heard this house has a fire suppression
system the whole way through it," I said wondering if the shock
of the earthquake had made him forgetful.

He stood up and started packing the bottles into a cardboard box on the loveseat. "Yep and there's one ginormous
Class BC fire extinguisher in Tony's office and another smaller
one in the kitchen. But I'm smelling a lot of fire around here.
I want to be prepared for anything."

"Right." I shrugged.

"And don't try to change the subject. I know you've got
a key to the front padlock and I think I know where it came
from, but it doesn't matter. You go AWOL again and I'll change
the lock. You can rot out there, see how much you like it on
the outside."

Ever since I'd got home he'd been cutting me with thin slices of guilt. I took it last night because I had screwed up but if I didn't push back today, I'd be under his thumb until Tony was back. When he looked at me with that arrogant gleam in his eye, I stared right back at him and said, "I'm staying because you've got a bad ankle."

Michael ran his fingers through his ruffled hair. It spiked out in every direction as if he had been doing that all night long. We glared at each other until I couldn't stand it any longer. His eyes were bloodshot and puffy and that was probably my fault too. I touched three fingers to my temple in a salute and said, "Dishonourable Sand Flea Rowan Morgan reporting for duty, Commander Michael, sir."

His lips twitched. With the crazies outside, we had enough to fight without battling each other. The same thought must have occurred to him and he let himself laugh. The tension between us evaporated like the dew on the lawn. Beside him on the table was an empty Coke can, a pair of binoculars, a blue exercise book and a pen.

I picked up the book. "Did you spend all night on the porch?"

"Pretty much."

"You could have seen from Tony's office."

"I like the peace, the privacy, of the middle of the night. Besides, the cameras only track what's going on around our house. I wanted to see the whole street."

"Anything worth seeing?" I flipped through the book. No notes. Just the date and time he came on shift.

"A family showed up just after midnight. Parents and a little kid, really young, two or three only. He had a scraped knee. They were picnicking in the park when the quake hit. Their car was destroyed. They waited all afternoon for a bus to get them home to Burnaby. Then they slept at a picnic shelter. Then they waited all day. I'm guessing there aren't going to be any buses for a while. They hadn't eaten since early yesterday so I gave them some granola bars, a bag of raisins, and a couple of bottles of water. I know I shouldn't have but no one was watching. They're walking down to the SeaBus to get home."

He had given away food, just like that. He made his own rules. It had been that way since I could remember, since I first saw him making popcorn when we were home alone on a Saturday afternoon. It was a Sometimes Food, which we weren't supposed to be eating without Mom or Tony being there. But Michael made up his own rules, even when we were nine and five. Back then Mom and Tony lived in the same house. They'd had another big fight and Mom had gone for a run in the pouring rain. Tony had burned off in his truck, Michael and I stood at the living room window and saw the two of them head out in opposite directions. Then Michael looked at me and said, "Popcorn!"

My job was to get the air freshener out of the bathroom and spray the whole house so Mom wouldn't smell it when she got back. Michael stood in front of the microwave and watched it pop. Then he lifted the package out carefully and spilled the contents into two bowls. Lion's share to him, a tiny portion for me.

"Hey," I said. "Not fair."

"That's because I'm the leader. Leaders always get more."

Almost ten years later and I had never totally shaken free of his so-called leadership. To him, I was still that same little kid. Just like Tony, he didn't ask me for my opinion because it didn't count.

I thought about him giving food away but I wasn't sure what was right or wrong any longer. Since Tony got hurt there seemed to be a curse on me breaking his rules. I left the compound and Michael twisted his ankle. Then something even worst almost happened to me. But nothing bad happened when Michael gave water to Javier and the Muellers or supplies to a young family. Maybe the curse was only on me, only on leaving the compound. Maybe Michael could do what he wanted. "What were they doing wandering around? Don't they know about the curfew?"

"They didn't and when I mentioned it they didn't seem to care. I told them how to get to Lynn Valley Road and said if they followed it downhill, they'd get to the SeaBus terminal eventually." He stacked his extinguisher components in a neat row in front of him and put the lid back on the vinegar jug.

"There're cops on Lynn Valley Road." I murmured and tried to imagine wandering around the darkness with a toddler and an empty belly. Half of me wanted to turn off the fence and throw open the gate. The other half wanted to add another padlock.

"I'm guessing when you've got no shelter and no food, being picked up by the cops might be a good deal." He rubbed his cheek. "After they left, I saw a bear at the far end of the cul-de-sac. I hope they stayed safe."

"Anything else?" I said. I checked the time: 7:03 AM. I wrote that in the book.

"One weird thing." Michael looked away like he didn't really want to tell me.

"Give it up," I said and locked my teeth together.

"I keep hearing that tune that dude in the forest was whistling."

"Hearing for real, or stuck-in-your-head-like-a-earworm hearing?"

"Hearing for real. At first I thought it was coming from the pedestrian path over near Jake's place. Then it seemed to be coming from the back of Kagome's house. I must be tired."

"Must be," I said. Michael had been suspicious of Greg. I hadn't told him how Greg appeared out of nowhere at Jake's house, then again at Wakeford Drive. No need to feed his irrational fears. Tony had enough for all of us.

Michael's gaze dropped to the ground. "Fact is I fell asleep twice. Both times I woke to that whistling and it was megacreepy. That's why I decided to make some fire extinguishers, to keep myself awake."

"Well now you can sleep in your own bed."

"How's Misty?" He tossed his Coke can into the box of extinguishers.

"Better. I've been bathing her cut in salted water. This morning there was no new blood at all. I'm going to keep her shut in my room though. I'm afraid if I let her out she'll run away. It'd be nice to give her back to the Kurtzes when they get home. You know, something that the earthquake didn't destroy."

"Don't worry, Rowanberry, we'll find Oliver. I know we will." Michael hadn't called me Rowanberry since elementary school. The softness of his voice reminded me of hiding under his desk together during thunderstorms when we were little. He used to whisper that I didn't need to worry because he'd protect me. I always knew he was as scared as I was but it didn't matter because I also knew the storm would end.

"And we'll be talking to Mom on the phone any minute now." Bitterness soured my voice so I added in a kinder tone, "I didn't think you'd worry so much when I went out. Sorry."

"I'm sorry too," he said. "I understand why you took off yesterday. Don't think I wasn't tempted to go too." He gave me a long, understanding look that I hadn't seen for years. It was warm and inclusive and I wanted to hang onto it with both hands. Before either of us could get sloppy or sentimental, he picked up his firefighting bombs and went inside.

I went down to the garden and opened the chicken house. The birds flapped out of their night roost hungry and squawking. I threw the feed on the ground and studied the huge yard. The house and fence stood solid while the rest of Tony's life stayed empty and barren. The rows of raised garden beds groaned under the abundance of late summer vegetables. People always thought the abundant crops were evidence of Tony's love of nature. False: it was all about his need for control.

Three crows landed on the Muellers' roof. One of them had something in its beak and the others tried to pull it away. Something furry and grey. Probably a squirrel. Road kill? Earthquake kill? I climbed the stairs and walked around the porch, searching for chickadees in the greenbelt on the far side of the house. I picked up a book and tried to read it but couldn't concentrate on the ridiculous fantasy world. I ran up and down the stairs to burn off some anxiety. I brought out the travel chess set and tried to get interested in the game for the millionth time.

Then I heard it. Half-growl, half-whine, something not quite human. A bead of cold sweat dribbled down my face. I ran up to the porch and yelled into the kitchen where Michael was making a pre-bedtime snack, "Michael."

There on the far corner of the fence, near the path to Jake's house, came a crawling figure. Too big for a dog or coyote, too small for a bear.

"What've you got?" Michael said, his voice sharp and alert. "There's something near the west fence. God, I think it's human."

CHAPTER 20 | RESCUE

NORTH VANCOUVER

The person moved closer on all fours. Seconds later Michael appeared at my side, his feet toed into undone hiking boots. He turned off the power on the fence and limped down the stairs. I followed. We slid through the gate and he locked it behind us before we edged closer.

As we approached the collapsed figure, it raised its head. I recognized the steel-framed glasses, even with one smashed lens. I looked again at the bruised and bloody face. Mrs. Patterson. Michael dropped on one knee beside her. I gawked at her torn and stained clothing.

"Mrs. Patterson? It's okay now, you're safe," Michael said, his tone low and calming. She crumpled against him and he turned to me. "We'll carry her in."

"Your ankle?"

"What else can we do? Ask Jake to help? Don't think so. He can't see his mom like this. Fireman's chair."

I tried not to hyperventilate. "Okay."

We crossed our arms and, without a word, Mrs. Patterson settled into the seat we made. She passed out almost immediately and I was reminded what the expression *dead weight* meant. She stank of blood and worse. I was thankful that years of hockey had strengthened my arms. Michael and I lugged her to the gate and set her down gently on the ground. I let her slump into me as Michael let us in. Then we hefted her up, carried her through and I crouched beside her as Michael made sure the gate was securely locked. She didn't stir the whole time and I wondered if that was because she trusted us implicitly or because she was close to death. I waited to find out. She didn't respond until we eased her into a chair in the guest room.

"Jacob," she croaked and pasty breath made me turn my head away.

"He's fine, Mrs. Patterson," Michael said. "He's staying here with us."

"Must see him." She placed her hands on the side of her chair like she wanted to stand.

"Let's get you ready, please, Mrs. Patterson. We're going to make up this bed for you but first we're going to put down a sheet until you're all cleaned up. Rowan, how about I stay with her? You get an old quilt."

I raced down to the laundry where Tony kept old clothing and bedding in cardboard boxes, all lined up like soldiers. Detailed inventory lists hung on the outside of each box. *Rubber sheets.* Just the thing to keep blood off the mattress. Tony thought of everything.

When I got back, Michael had the first aid kit out and was laying bandages in a row on the night table. Linda moaned as we lifted her onto the bed. "That hurts so much," she said almost inaudibly as I took her sandals off.

"Where?" Michael asked.

"Everywhere," she whimpered. "Jacob?"

"He's okay, Mrs. Patterson." My turn to reassure her. "He's here, downstairs sleeping."

She looked at me through swollen, blackened eyes.

"Get him, please." Her words drooped. I forced myself to not to turn away. She was crusted with dirt and I could barely tell the injuries from the filth. A brown circle of dried blood radiated out from her shoulder and over her chest. One arm was scratched. Not a small Misty-sized scratch but a big ugly wound. Her bare feet were black and swollen and her hair poked out from her head like highlighted thorns.

"Give me a minute and then get Jake," Michael whispered. "But first, turn the fence back on." He smoothed her hair off her face and looked at the bruises around her eyes. "Mrs. Patterson we'll get Jake for you but he's kind of sensitive. Before he gets here, I'd like to wash your face, tidy you up a bit, if that's okay."

She nodded and smiled weakly at him. "Okay. Please call me Linda."

Call me Linda? Okay then I could call her Linda too. I guess we were all BF's now.

"Michael, you have to rest." I whispered. "You're limping really badly."

"Don't worry about me. Just turn on the fence before some of our feral neighbours decide to help themselves to the last of the garden. Then get Tony's hiking stick. I think she's going to need it."

When I returned with the improvised cane, Michael was bringing a bucket of water out of the bathroom. A package of disposable cloths and a biohazard bag lay next to the bandages on the night table.

"Isn't that kind of overkill?" I indicated the autoclave bag.

"When do you think would be the right time to use one?" he asked as he pulled on disposable rubber gloves. He dipped a cloth into the water, wrung it out and started to gently sponge

Linda's face. She lay so still I thought she might have passed out.

Not knowing what to say, I studied the photo on the wall. It was one of Tony's shots of Cheakamus Lake last fall. A tree with red and yellow leaves framed the lake and the snow-capped mountain in the background. It was all so tranquil and part of a different lifetime.

Michael stared at me, waiting for an answer. I shrugged. "For bloody bandages from someone we *don't* know? I doubt Linda has AIDS or anything."

"Blood is full of microorganisms. I'm not taking any chances. The whole world could be back to normal tomorrow. If it's not and we have to help any other injured people, do we want to have a lot of bloody rags mixed in with our regular garbage? Get Jake up but don't bring him in here until I'm ready."

I shut the door behind me and thought about the word "normal." I had seen the destroyed houses of the neighbourhood. How long had it taken for Tony to build this house? How long had it taken for the normal houses on Clonmel Place to be built? Months. Years. How many houses had I seen that that needed fixing or even rebuilding? The new normal could be this, being locked in this house and this yard, helping people as best we could. Not helping other people when it would put our own survival at risk. I hoped Tony had lots more biohazard bags in his war chest.

Jake slept on top of his covers, wearing only a pair of boxers. His limbs were flung in wild directions and he looked like a stick man with one extra stick. *Get a boner shield, please.* Flushed with embarrassment, I bumped his shoulder and turned my back.

"Mom?"

I shivered and thought about his mom's injuries. I thought how I would feel if mine turned up in the same condition. Poor Jake. "Wake up," I said.

"Row? Wh-what's happening?"

My nick, the name that only family and friends used, sounded soft and right coming from him, as if he'd been calling me that for years. "Please get up, Jake."

"What is it?"

"Get dressed, please." I heard him yawn. His feet hit the floor. "Your mom, she's back. But she's been hurt." I said and turned back to him.

"No!" He made a beeline toward the door, shirt in one hand, jeans in the other.

"Wait." I caught his arm and felt the flex of his muscles as he resisted me. I hadn't noticed how broad his shoulders were before.

"Stop. Get dressed okay? Then brace yourself." I locked his eyes with mine. I wanted him to know he had a friend who would help him no matter what. "I don't know what happened to her but she's pretty beaten up. Michael is helping her. He says for us to wait outside. He'll let you know when she's ready to see you."

Jake nodded, tight-lipped, and took his clothes into the bathroom. After a long, long time he came out, pale-faced. He rummaged through his backpack and brought out a glasses case. "Does she need these?" he asked.

"Glasses?"

"Spare ones. I got them when I got my guitar."

"Hers are broken. How'd you know?"

"Didn't but she's bat blind. She keeps spare glasses stashed everywhere so I just grabbed one on my way out of the house."

As we sat on the front porch and waited, both of us stretching our ears toward the dark hallway for Michael's signal, music drifted over the morning quiet. *The Gypsy Rover.* Jake spun around and yelled, "Greg."

As if by magic there he was, just outside the gate, his hands in his pockets. Yesterday's five o'clock shadow had bloomed to a short beard. Without his orange baseball cap, I might not have recognized him. He carried a pack with a first aid kit logo on the top of it. Jake and I charged down to see him.

"Greg. My mom's been hurt I don't know how badly."

"Badly," I mouthed.

Greg rocked back on his heels for a minute as if he was thinking about what to do. Then his face relaxed and he said, "Can I help? Of course you'd have to let me through this gate first."

He looked at me and my face burned. It felt as if he was x-raying my brain and could sense all my suspicious thoughts about him. Still, his training aced anything Michael and I got in the windowless rooms of St. John Ambulance.

I pursed my lips to show Greg I was still undecided. Then I turned and said, "Jake, could you please turn off the power."

When he gave the all clear, I unlocked the gate. Greg slipped in and I waited until Jake signalled that the power was back on before I invited Greg into the house.

"What happened to her?" Greg asked. His tone was brusque, detached like a mathematician.

"I don't know. She hasn't talked hardly at all. Her glasses are smashed, she's got big scratches, and there's blood around her shoulder."

"She's in luck. I have a full bag of supplies here. Saline, sutures and sealing wax."

I smiled at his attempt at humour. We sure needed some. Greg patted Jake's shoulder and that small act of reassurance reached me too.

Inside, I tapped once on the guest room door. Michael and Linda whispered a bit before Michael called out, "Come in."

Linda was covered with a sheet up to her neck and Michael knelt beside her. She had her right arm on top of the sheet and flinched as Michael irrigated one of the deep scratches. When Michael saw Greg, he did a double take. Before I could say a thing, Jake pushed past Michael and dropped to his knees in front of his mother.

"Jacob," she said.

He wrapped his arms around her and held on tight. He didn't see the pain that registered on her face. "Mom, you okay?"

"Seeing you in one piece just made me feel one hundred percent better. I'm going to be okay now." Her weak laugh ended in a cough.

Michael looked at the medic bag in Greg's hand and relaxed. "The pro is here."

He stood back and waved Greg to Linda's side.

"I'm Greg Phillips," he said with a bright smile. "I'm a paramedic. May I help you? Mrs...?"

"Patterson. Linda Patterson. Jacob's mother. Yes, please. I think I could use some help," Linda said. Her voice sounded fainter than a second ago. "Jacob and I live in the house behind this one, on the next street over. Or at least we used to."

"You mean the house where Jake turned off the gas?" Greg dug in his first aid bag and brought out a penlight.

"Jacob did what?" Linda didn't attempt to hide her disbelief. She swallowed hard and peered at Greg. "You remind me of someone. Do I know you?"

"Doubt it. I'm from Alberta." He held her wrist and checked his watch. "I think we need to get these rags off you so we can clean your wounds properly. Rowan, do you have anything that might fit Linda?"

"Uh huh," I said but didn't move.

"Do you know what day it is, Linda?" He examined one of her eyes and then the other.

"Not sure exactly. Thursday? Which part of Alberta?" Her voice paled on the word Alberta.

"It's Friday. Linda, I think you may have a serious concussion, which means you really need to rest. I promise to tell you my life story when you're a bit stronger. Rowan, clothes?"

I stopped staring and clapped my mouth shut. I always thought Mrs. Patterson—Linda—was an iron lady. Mr. Patterson travelled a lot so she managed everything house. She didn't do the work herself but when the service came to mow their lawn or shovel their driveway, she marched up and down, spouting orders like a five-star general. Most of the people in the neighbourhood liked her because she knew who to phone at the District offices if you had a complaint about the garbage truck coming too early or someone's cat getting into your garden.

I was the exception. I didn't like her and I made sure she didn't like me the first time I met her. When they moved in three years ago, I hoped that the new boy in the 'hood might become my friend for the summer months when I was doomed to live at Tony's. A few days after the moving truck left, Michael and I were playing shinny hockey in the cul-de-sac. Only two other kids had joined us and they were both hopeless players. I decided Jake might be the answer so I knocked on the Pattersons' door and asked if he'd like to join us.

Linda looked me up and down as if she had never seen a girl in goalie pads before. She sniffed like she smelled something bad before she said, "No, Jacob does not play hockey. He's not even permitted to watch blood sports."

"It's not a blood sport," I argued.

"Well it's far too violent for a young girl like you. Do your parents know what you're up to?"

Her death-ray eyes tried to level me but instead they ignited a flare of anger. Before I could stop myself, I retaliated with war words. "They not only know but my dad comes to every one of my games. He's not a lame helicopter parent, hovering over me every minute of my life."

That was a lie. After my silent months Tony watched me like a science experiment. For the longest time, when I stayed at his house, I had to be in his yard, with him, or with Michael. He encouraged me to do the sports he loved but that was the most freedom I knew at his place, and he went to every game and every practice. He drove me to and from my friends' houses so I wouldn't have to take the bus.

Mom accepted the fact that I had finally recovered from the assault but Tony never did. Linda's comments cut close to the bone and I did what any good hockey forward would have done—I played offense.

As I thumped down the steps in my rollerblades, I smiled to myself. I had never spoken to an adult like that before and it felt amazing. Not for a single second did I consider that once I'd blown her off that way, I could never make peace. The toothpaste was out of the tube. I didn't care. Not then anyway. Now that I knew Jake better, it might be nice if his mom and I could be friendlier but that wasn't going to happen soon.

I studied her and considered for the first time how petite she was, probably six inches shorter than me and at least two, maybe three, sizes smaller. "Tony's got a lot of old clothes in the basement. Maybe there's something in there from when I was younger. Greg, would you like anything?"

Greg pulled a blood pressure cuff out of his bag and wound it around Linda's upper arm. "Water, but not now. And that's a fine looking garden you've got. When we're done here, I'd be grateful for a salad and some fruit. In the meantime I think you young people should leave Michael and me alone with Linda."

He said her name easily, with care and concern. He didn't use that tone with me when I was practically raped, almost killed, by the gang the day before. That's the problem with being able to take care of yourself. No one ever thinks you need help. I slouched toward the door.

"Okay, you young people heard the professional here." Michael couldn't sound more arrogant if he tried and I wished that Greg hadn't included him in the professional care circle. On the bed Linda breathed, slow and shallow. Jake's face drained of colour so before he could panic, I dragged him out of there.

When Greg and Michael emerged from the guest room, I was showered, with my brushed hair draped over my shoulders, soft and shiny. I wore my best cargo shorts and a pale green baby-doll tee. It felt like I'd washed away some of the disaster and worry that had been clinging to me for two days.

"Did the clothes fit?" I asked. I couldn't believe that Tony had kept every single thing both Michael and I had put in the bag for the charity shop, back when we were changing sizes and styles every year. Some of those clothes dated back to the age of dinosaurs. That left a choice between everything pink and purple—my favourite colours through grades seven and eight—or Michael's castoffs from elementary school. I wondered how she liked super hero T-shirts. I had taken her a stack from both our collections.

"Yeah but I bet she's never dressed like that before. You used to wear really bright shorts." Michael swung the autoclave bag around.

"What're you going to do with that?" I pointed to the bag.

"Burn it," he smiled. Burning things was one of his favourite pastimes.

"Best thing for it," Greg added. "We don't want a lot of biowaste lying around. Michael says you've got an incinerator?"

Michael put his hand on the back door, "Greg would you like to catch a rest here? That way if Linda needs help, you'll be here for her?"

"Yeah." I said, trying to break Michael's stranglehold on favour giving. "You could even have a shower."

"A shower?" Greg grinned.

"A short shower," Michael said. "Three minutes max. There're timers in all the bathrooms."

"My mother didn't raise a fool—I couldn't say no to an offer like that." Greg winked at me and I smiled with satisfaction. "I'm not due back at the ambulance depot until evening. Yeah, I'd like to crash here for a bit if that's okay with you."

Michael collected a book of matches and tin of lighter fluid from under the sink and disappeared outside. At the table Jake picked at his toast and honey. Greg sat down and smiled, "Your mom's resting now but she's going to be fine. She's still pretty concussed and needs to be in a quiet, dark room for a while, probably a couple of days. The best thing you can do is show her that you're healthy and well so that she can stop worrying about you. That'll help her recover faster than anything."

Jake nodded and sat a little straighter.

Greg picked up a pear from the bowl in the centre of the table. "Your mother should buy a lottery ticket when all this is over. She couldn't have arrived here at a better time. I had just dropped a patient down the street a ways when I saw you kids come up on the porch." He bit into the pear, a tiny careful bite and his nose twitched as he chewed slowly. "I had everything Linda needed physically in my pack. You had everything she needed emotionally in the shape of one young man. She's going to be fine. I'll watch over her for a while just to be sure."

I left the two of them talking and sat on the back stairs where I could see Michael in the yard below. The smell of lighter fluid reached me one minute and the warmth of the fire the next. The flames in the metal drum licked high into the air. The last of the blood-soaked rags were fed into the fire and the smoke streaked over the trees behind the house before it faded into the sky.

Where was Mom? She was smart, much smarter than Tony. She'd be okay. She had to be. I shoved that razor-toothed torment into the worry box and slammed down the lid. As I did that, more dark clouds flew out. I missed Tony big time. I missed his certainty about what was black and what was white. I missed the way he knew just want to do in emergencies. I wondered how long he would have to stay in the hospital. I wished Oliver would show up, safe and sound, so there would be one less worry in my world. My eyes tracked the smoke. I thought about how Greg had turned up like a miracle when we needed one. Maybe there were more miracles in store.

CHAPTER 21 | FIELD SURGERY

VANCOUVER, WEST END

The surgeon checked Dixie's pulse and breathing. She injected a powerful local anaesthetic into the leg before administering a second shot of strong opiates. Almost immediately Dixie sailed into the clouds. She closed her eyes and welcomed the weightlessness. Then she opened them again and peered into the harsh light of the emergency beacon. Voices reached her from far away.

"Help," she tried to say but the word stuck in her throat. Before she could try again, the drugs carried her back to the land of happy and her worries evaporated.

The next thing she knew, Dr. Singh lay beside her, gloved and gowned. "Hi, Dixie. I'm ready now, are you?" The mask muffled her words and made her sound a thousand miles away. Perspiration poured down her face.

"You're not claustrophobic are you?" Dixie tried to joke.

Dr. Singh shook her head. "Dixie, I'm going to make an incision above your knee, okay? Then I will isolate the muscles before I amputate. After I close the muscles over the stump, they'll be covered with skin and I'll dress it. Then we'll get you out of here and Dr. Harrison will make you much more comfortable. You just need to hang on for the next hour or so okay? It'll be smooth sailing after that."

Dixie smiled and nodded at Dr. Singh. The morphine had made her tongue thick and useless. But she was brave, no one could argue that. She'd had two children by natural childbirth. And a few years ago, on the West Coast Trail, she slipped on a mossy ladder and twisted her ankle. She hiked out to the next evacuation spot across miles of rough terrain. By the time she reached Carmanah Point her mild injury had deteriorated to a Grade Three sprain. The agony had been blinding. She had managed it without humiliating herself. She could handle anything.

Her mind wandered. She was on that hike again, watching the whales breach off Owen Point. *How many people get to see that?* The pain getting home had been totally worth it.

She didn't feel the first cut of the scalpel. When the muscles were divided and the blood vessels clamped, her resolve weakened. She whimpered. Then the saw ground and bit against her femur. It shrieked ten times worse than any dental drill. The tiny cave trapped the shrill whine and magnified it until it deafened her. The steel sliced through solid bone. Severed nerve endings ignited waves of pain that no drug could stop. The metallic smell of blood filled the air. A crimson haze of terror wrapped around her and her determination shattered. She screamed. She screamed until her voice failed. Then darkness carried her away again.

Glimmers of consciousness came and went. First she was dragged out of the long dark tunnel. Dust rained down on her and people spoke in urgent, disjointed voices. She was on a board, fastened to it in a hundred places, with a block around her head. Someone held her hand. A female voice said, "It's okay now, Dixie, the worst is over." A constellation of pain strobed in her vision. A man, who was at least three hundred years old, took her blood pressure while a woman hooked up an IV on her left wrist.

"I'm Dr. Harrison," the man said, "you're going to be fine." He called orders to the nurse in what sounded like a foreign language. Another sedative bloomed in her veins and Dixie slipped back to the warm beach on the Pacific Ocean.

She woke in the back of an SUV and two worried faces watched over her from the front seat. Red rays of sunset flecked the sky as she was carried somewhere. The football stadium? The hot air drooped with humidity. At the end of her gurney the petite doctor wept. Two other women joined her. They talked quietly and then without warning they all laughed. Dr. Singh wiped her cheeks. The blond one with the thick eyebrows lifted the thin blanket and looked at Dixie's stump. The one with a lab coat over her yoga-wear brushed the hair from Dixie's mouth. She smelled of coffee.

"Dixie? How are you? I'm Dr. Emily Walter, I'm a surgeon who works with Dr. Singh when she'll let me. Harminder has done an excellent job on your leg. We'll have you up and walking in no time." Her hand felt cool and dry as she stroked Dixie's forehead.

Tears leaked down Dixie's face and she stifled her sobs.

Many hours later Dixie woke again. The retractable roof loomed hundreds of feet above her. *Why hadn't it collapsed?*

"How are you feeling, dear?" A young man leaned over her. He wore a stethoscope around his neck, a facemask, and a headlamp in the middle of his forehead

"Hurts."

"You're in luck." He reached over her head and tapped the IV feed to her wrist. "We have pain medication today."

Dixie looked away as he prepared a syringe. She wondered how her family was. Were Michael and Rowan safe? Did they know where she was and what had happened? Were they searching for her? In the dim glow of the emergency lights she saw rows of people spread out around her, some on stretchers, some on gurneys, some on blankets on the ground. People with bandaged limbs and faces. Some wailed and wept. Some lay as still as corpses. They all had names and mothers and fathers and sons and daughters and lovers and friends. Would families ever be reunited?

CHAPTER 22 | HIGH HOPES

NORTH VANCOUVER

Later that night, when Greg had left for work, I cornered Michael as he started his midnight sentry duty.

"I think we should invite Greg to stay as long as he wants," I said.

"Why?" Michael raised an eyebrow.

"Because Tony's really sick. Greg could help him come home from the hospital sooner."

"Greg's not a nurse you know."

"I know that. But he is medically trained. He could teach us how to look after Tony. You and me've only got basic first aid. Besides I bet if Tony has a choice between staying in the hospital surrounded by disease and strangers or coming home where there is only one stranger, a paramedic to boot, he'll want to come home."

Michael shrugged. "Might. I guess as long as Greg's here we've still got the option. I'll invite him to stay for now, as long as he looks after Linda. Besides with me being half lame because of my ankle, I'm guessing it won't hurt to have one more able-bodied person inside."

There must have been a miscommunication in the invitation because at breakfast the next morning Greg took over as commanding officer.

"Our days are very changed now," he said in a pay-attention kind of way. "The increments that used to divide our lives, time with friends, work, study, going for a hike, watching TV, those things are gone for now."

"Your father's right," he said with a meaningful glance at me, "you *should* all stay in the compound. Even when the curfew comes off you should wait until the roads are passable and emergency services can cope again. When it's chaos all around us, it's even more important to structure our lives and to try to stay as healthy as we can. And the compound must be kept safe."

Michael grunted in agreement. Then, as he mopped the last of his eggs up with a piece of toast, he said, "I gotta remind you, Greg, that once Linda's out of danger, you may have to leave. Everyone but family may have to leave. I've got no problem with three more people here but Tony may have a different opinion." Michael's eyes were still red-rimmed and I wondered how anyone sleeping so much could look so tired.

Greg crunched a piece of bacon. "I'm grateful to stay as long as you're willing to have me. If Tony doesn't want me here, I'll leave. No problem. We can cross that bridge when we come to it."

That morning an army truck pulled up at the end of the cul-de-sac and handed out water and rations. I sat with Jake and saw the neighbours walk back with small bags of food. For a moment I felt as if I were floating, as if the world was coming back to normal. The wolf stepped back from their doors for another day and they could stay away from us, for now.

Sunday morning, three days after she'd found her way to our place, Linda emerged from her cave. It was my shift and I was sitting in the office watching the CCTV monitors as she shuffled past. She leaned gingerly on Tony's hiking stick, as if she expected the ground below her to give way at any time. Her wet hair hung in a flat, thin fringe around her face. Dark-rimmed glasses made her appear severe, more disapproving than ever. I jumped up and followed her to see the grand entrance into the kitchen. My old mini dress showed off her long, slender legs. I saw the way Greg checked them out and decided he was a pervert.

"Mom," Jake said as she approached. He pretended to wipe his mouth with a napkin but I knew he was spitting out his gum. Clever move, Jake-boy.

Linda peered around the room. "Jacob, would you please get me a drink of water." She lowered herself gently onto a chair. Until this week, I'd never seen her without her hair puffed up, a load of makeup, and a king's ransom in jewellery. She seemed frail, smaller, like a knight without armour.

Greg stood back from the sink where he was washing dishes. "Linda, it's good to see you up and about."

Good to see her? She was one big rainbow-coloured bruise from head to foot. The marks around her eyes were purplish-black but the bruises on her bare legs and arms were still the ugly red-blue of a fresh injury. *She looks like she's been in a really bad hockey fight*, I thought with a twinge of sympathy.

"I don't know for how long," Linda said in a poor-me voice. "But I think I should start to have my meals with everyone else, help out where I can."

"By all means," Greg said. "But take it carefully for the first day or so, okay?"

"I will, but with Tony in the hospital, these children need supervising." She gazed at me like a cat staring down a mouse.

She turned a much sweeter face to Greg. "I realize you're doing the best you can, Greg, but you have to work and I'll be here all the time, at least until Tony gets back."

I wished Michael were there with me, to tell her we weren't kids. He was old enough to drink and vote. He didn't need her telling him what to do. But Michael was sleeping again. When he told Greg that he was lead-limbed tired all the time, Greg said that wasn't unusual after the shock of the earthquake. Still, it would have been nice if he were there when I needed him.

I started to speak but Greg got in first, like I needed his defence. "These children, as you call them, are more responsible than many so-called adults. They'd been on their own for days, with their father in the hospital and no idea of where their mother is or their friends are and they didn't sit around and feel sorry for themselves. They did what everyone else should've done; they took care of the home front. That's why there are fresh vegetables in the fridge and bowls of berries for breakfast. You'll find it very easy to work with them."

His voice was casual and she nodded. Some secret message passed between the two of them. She rubbed a torn cuticle and looked up at me. A chill raced down my neck. I'd let an enemy into the house. I tightened my grip on my water glass and wanted to say something that would make her think twice about trying to take over. Only my mind blanked so I tossed my head.

"Jacob, make me some toast, please." She didn't ask, she ordered.

Jake shrugged like it didn't matter, but his neck stiffened and red spots burned his cheeks. He jumped to his feet and pushed a slice of bread into the toaster.

"Excuse me," Linda said in the tone I might have used on a naughty five-year-old. "Did you clean out the crumb tray first? Now set it on light, I want my bread only just toasted, not burnt. Honestly Jacob, haven't I taught you anything?"

As spoke, she turned an angry face to me, as if I were the reason Jake wasn't doing what things the way she wanted. My sense of contentment withered and died.

After her brief royal appearance, Linda took her cloud of crankiness back to bed. Greg hung around and helped me with the rest of the dishes. I waited until Jake was back on the porch doing his watch before I spoke. "So Linda is getting much better."

Greg took the plate and dried it. "Yeah, she may not need me around as much. I might be able to spend more time helping out at the shelters and hospital."

Hope sparked in my chest. "Do you think they'll let you in to see Tony? Could you take him a note?"

"I can try. I know they still aren't letting any visitors in but I should be able to get past security with my paramedic clearance. Give me your note and I'll see what I can do. I'll tell him that I'm staying here with Jake and his mom. That way he'll know that you're not on your own."

I plunged my hands into the dishwater and stared at the soap bubbles as they sighed quiet pops.

"No." I shook my head and tried to keep the panic out of my voice. "That might not be a very good idea. He's majorly suspicious and you'll have to be really careful about what you say."

"Okay how about I say that you have a neighbour staying with you with some serious injuries and that you let me help her. I don't have to tell him I'm staying here."

"No. No. No. That's way too much information. Tony'll flip if he hears there are outsiders staying here. You don't know him. I do." I wrung the dishcloth in my hands and wrestled with the part of me that wanted to know, really and truly, how Tony was. It would be a federal offence if I finagled my way in to see him but if Greg Nobody showed up and started telling a lot of half-truths Tony'd explode. He could smell a lie from outer space and Michael and I would be on our way to the hanging tree. My breath came in ragged gulps at the thought of Tony's reaction. Should I just trust the system instead? Besides Tony was strong. *As tough as old boot leather* according to Mom. I'd never even seen him sick with the flu. What could be safer than a hospital bed?

Greg slid the last plate on top of the pile in the cupboard and turned to me. "Trust me, Rowan, I'll be careful and I'll gauge the situation better in person."

His strong dark eyes held mine but I shook my head. "No, you can't. Please."

He was wrong, all wrong. Everything was wrong now. I wished it were Tony standing beside me, instead of Greg. I wanted it to be Tony so that he could hold me like he did when I was a kid, stroke my hair and make the darkness go away. When Greg touched my arm, the image of Tony disappeared and I was looking into the face of a stranger.

Voices erupted at the front of the house. Jake shouted, "You're not getting anything so you may as well go away."

"Where's Tony Morgan? You tell him to get out here and tell us to our faces that he's going to let us starve."

I recognized Don Redgrave's voice as Greg and I ran to the porch. A dozen people crowded the front of the fence. Greg stopped at the top of the stairs and faced them.

"My name is Greg Phillips. How can I help you?"

"Food. We need some," Don Redgrave demanded.

These people were not going to take over Tony's home. I swaggered down the stairs to the gate, determined to set the record straight. My hands shook and I forced out the first words that came to me, "The army gave you rations. Why're you here? Go home."

Don Redgrave kept talking to Greg up on the porch. I felt invisible.

"We're trying to take care of our families. We hardly got any supplies at all. What we got is all gone," Don Redgrave said, his voice angry and demanding. "Now let us talk to that fruitloop Morgan."

"I'm Tony's friend," Greg said. "Whatever you want to say to him, you can say to me."

"And whatever you say to Greg you can say to me," I said. Everyone ignored me.

Greg continued as if I'd said nothing. "Even if we've got anything to share, and I'm not saying we do, we won't be sharing with a mob. The worse you behave, the more entrenched our position will become. Is this clear?"

"I don't know how you can sleep at night, letting people starve." Don Redgrave said. He looked at the people around him and they shouted at us in a noisy chorus.

"The Muellers said you gave them water," Cindy Redgrave said.

"What about us?" A woman with a poodle haircut at the back called out. I'd never seen her before.

We couldn't take care of the world. That should be obvious.

The crowd continued to mutter and complain. The heat of the sun was pale compared to their tempers. They stank of fever, the same hysteria fever that hung in the air outside the hospital.

"Under the Emergency Program Act we can seize your food and water and distribute it to those who need it," said poodle-cut. I wondered how she knew so much about the Act, but not enough to have prepared better.

"You don't have the authority to do that," Greg said but everyone ignored him as this new information rippled through the crowd.

They answered with howls and jeers. Some started chanting, "Food! Food! Food!"

Greg put his fingers in his mouth and whistled loud and shrill. When everyone stopped talking he said, "Go home, people. I don't know what you've heard about this house but we don't have all that much on hand ourselves. We're likely to run out in a few days anyway."

That was a pathetic lie. People could see right in at our garden and count the rows of lettuces, carrots and beets. The tomato plants bent under the fullness of their fruit. I stepped back from the fence and moved closer to Greg. I wanted everyone's eyes on me, not on the garden beds that were bursting with vegetables and berries.

Greg kept talking. "How about everyone keep their heads? If there isn't more coming through the emergency channels in a couple of days, then we'll see what we have to spare."

My jaw dropped and I gawked at him, bug-eyed. *WTH?* What gave him the right to promise our food? I looked at these people—some of them complete strangers, some of them neighbours I'd known for years. Some wore dirty, creased clothing, the clothes they were wearing on the day of the quake.

I wanted to share. I felt like we were harbouring bottomless riches. We should haul all those second-hand clothes up from the basement and give them to whoever needed them. We had lots of bottled water, powdered milk, tins of stew and macaroni dinners. We could put together some care packages. It would be better to help a few people than no one at all.

But it wasn't Greg's decision to offer anything to anyone.

I thought about Tony and the fact that he would be home any day. He needed to be part of the decision-making process, whatever we did next. He knew about emergencies and he was the only one who could say when it was time to open up the food safe.

Outside the fence, people whispered a bit. Don Redgrave, the self-appointed boss, said, "Two days. Two days only. Holding onto food when others go hungry is damned near criminal and if we don't have anything by Tuesday, we're coming in to take it ourselves."

I climbed the stairs slowly, wondering how we would talk away the trouble when everybody came back in two days. We'd think of something, Michael and me. When I joined Greg on the porch, he said, "This is a little earlier than I expected."

"What is?" I asked.

"Hysteria. Jealousy. Retribution. A lot of crap." He shook his head and a shadow of worry flashed across his face.

"Some of those people seem really hungry though," I said. I forced myself not to look over my shoulder at them. "Some of them are almost dressed in rags."

"I know, Rowan, but all those people had a chance to prepare themselves. Don't you have programs in school that teach you about emergency preparation?"

"We do."

"And doesn't the government advertise the need to be ready for disasters?"

"It does."

"So it's kind of like that fable about the little red hen. None of those people chose to do anything to prepare themselves but now they all want to take what isn't theirs. Right?"

"I suppose."

Jake had the rocking chair and Greg leaned on one side of the front door. I leaned on the other side and watched the crowd. I wondered if I should go downstairs and wake up Michael. Tell him what was happening and ask if he thought we should give away some of Tony's emergency supplies.

As if he read my mind Greg said, "There's another problem in all this too."

"Yeah?"

"If a mob gets inside those gates, there's always the risk that someone will grab more than they need, more than we're offering. Some greedy person might snatch something off someone else. It only takes one or two people to panic and it'll be a riot. As long as we can, we have to try to keep them on the other side of the fence."

Jake's eyebrows knit together and he fanned his hands. Before he got too anxious I said, "We can handle them. It's not the first time they've been around. They're all bark."

"You're right, Rowan." Greg said. "Every time they show up we'll turn them away. Eventually they'll get tired of asking."

My feelings churned like oil and water. I wanted the sense of safety with another person in the house but I didn't trust Greg, not entirely. He slipped into the us-and-them mode a little too easily, as if he belonged in the compound, making decisions about our food and water that weren't his to make.

A small aftershock rattled the ground and people on the street stopped rigid and frightened. A couple glowered back at the compound as if we might have caused it.

"How many is that now?" Jake asked.

"Lots. Too many to count," I said. The Redgraves walked back to their house but I didn't trust them. I faced Greg. "You're going to leave us here with them out there?"

"Leave?" Jake echoed.

"You know I've got to go to work and I need to get an update on Rowan's dad." He looked at me and I scorched him with my eyes. I didn't know what I wanted him to do but I sure didn't want him talking to Tony.

"I won't talk to Tony, I promise," Greg said and put his hand over his heart. "I'll speak to his doctors if I can."

"But if the neighbours see you leave, won't they try to break in or something?" I said. "They've got to have figured out Tony isn't home. If he was, he'd be parading around the yard like a peacock. Proud of how ready he is. Happy at how unready everyone else is."

One of the stragglers from the crowd walked back to the fence and called, "C'mon in there. How about some water, just a little bit?"

"We're running low ourselves," I shouted. "Drain your hot water tank."

"Bitch," the man said but he turned and walked away. I glanced at Greg as if to say *what did I tell you?*

"Keep the fence live. It'll deter most people. Under no circumstances let anyone know how much water and food you've got. It sounds as if they know too much already. Am I clear?" Greg spoke mostly to Jake and I yawned. I didn't like him telling me what to do in my own house. I guessed I was more like

Tony than I realized. Not looking at either of us, Jake stood and bounced on his heels.

"Okay, the show's just begun now, Jake. Are you okay to keep watch?"

Jake sat down and rocked. He jerked his head yes and squared his shoulders.

"That's the way." Greg smiled. "How about I join you for a while? Could you show me a few tunes on that guitar of yours. Can you play it?"

"Yes." Jake smiled and the rocker slowed. "I'll go get it."

"Good. Rowan and I will do a perimeter check and meet you back here."

While Jake was gone, Greg looked around before he spoke. "I've got a plan but it has to be our secret, okay? I'm not going to leave by the front gate. I want to turn off the fence and isolate a section of it that will not be electrified, near the greenbelt at the back. Wanna help?"

I didn't know what he was thinking but it was obvious that he was going back to the hospital with or without my approval. I shrugged. "Sure, I guess."

Greg whispered, "We'll cut an entrance there and isolate it from the power grid. It won't be electrified but it'll be padlocked like the one out front. Only you and I can know about this okay? It'll be perfectly secure but don't tell anyone. Loose lips and all that. The bushes in the park on the other side of the fence will hide our handiwork."

"Okay," I said. "As long as this is our secret. We tell no one else."

As we picked up tools in the garage, I thought of how useful a secret entrance could be. Cut through the biting canes of the blackberry thicket, it would be almost impenetrable if you didn't know the exact route—the perfect way to bring Tony home. No one needed to know Tony had been sick in the first place. It was a good idea.

After the secret gate had been cut into the fence and the power turned back on again, Greg and I joined Jake on the porch
"Any more crowd control problems?" Greg asked, scanning the street.

"A couple of kids came around. I said our supplies were running low and they went away." Jake snapped open the latches on the guitar case. He spoke quietly and way too casually. I didn't believe a word of it.

"Good work," Greg said. "You'll be ready for a job in emergency services any day now."

A small smile crossed Jake's face as he lifted the guitar out of its green, crushed-velvet cocoon.

"Nice axe, man," Greg said.

"Do you play?"

"A little," Greg said.

"Here, try it. It's got amazing tone."

Greg examined it. "Wow. A Martin D-28. A Marquis no less."

"You know it?" Jake asked, grinning at Greg's attention. I noticed that Jake didn't bother explaining how it was his father's. He wanted Greg to believe he bought himself and I understood. We all want to reinvent ourselves.

"Know of it is more like it," Greg said. "Johnny Cash played Martins most of his life. This is one pretty rare beast." With that he strummed a few chords and the quick sure movements of his fingers mesmerized me.

When a deep bass-baritone voice chimed in with *Folsom Prison Blues* I looked up at Greg only it wasn't Greg singing, it was Jake. His eyes were closed and he sang with controlled but powerful emotion. The act of singing transformed him. He was soulful, almost hot. Greg added his voice and at the end of the song he handed the guitar back to Jake. "It's been a lot of years since I played. My fingers are too soft for it now."

"Until I moved in here, I played almost every day. I didn't want to bug anyone with the noise," Jake said, his head bent over the instrument as if he were apologizing.

"Do you know any more Johnny Cash?" Greg asked.

A grin split Jake's face. "I know all of it."

Jake's playing was confident and sounded flawless to me. They encouraged me to add my weak voice to their two strong ones. I sang very quietly as they blended their voices like a second instrument. Their phrasing was similar, as if they communicated without words. It reminded me of how Michael and Javier spoke to each other, with a telepathic language that excluded me. If I were to vaporize at that very moment, they wouldn't notice for another hour or more.

A door slammed in the house and angry footsteps marched down the hallway. Linda had made a rapid recovery.

"Jacob." She bellowed from behind the screen door. "Stop that racket." She shot daggers at me as if I was the problem. She looked more human than she did the first day she arrived but I wasn't fooled. Inside she was still a Rowan-hating monster.

"Try to have some consideration for other people," she added. "Some of us are trying to rest."

"Mom, we're just trying to lighten the mood a bit." Jake's voice sounded tense, annoyed. I'd never heard him challenge her before.

Her cheeks reddened and she said, "Don't you dare talk back to me, young man." With one hard last hard stare, she huffed back into the house.

I clapped one hand over my mouth and with the other made a cut-throat motion across my neck. Greg and Jake laughed quietly. Jake's eyes met mine for a second and we nodded at each other. Something much greater than music had just happened on that porch.

CHAPTER 23 | SKELETONS

NORTH VANCOUVER

The next night, Greg came home for dinner. He found me in the kitchen, stirring a mushroom risotto. It was a special thank you meal because he was going to bring news about Tony.

"How's Tony?" I asked, studying his face.

"Still very weak." He went to the sink and washed his hands, his back turned.

A sick feeling wrenched me. "You didn't talk to him, did you?"

"No, I promised I wouldn't. Besides he was sleeping. I'll go again tomorrow."

"What's the hospital like? Could he come home? We could take care of him here couldn't we?"

"No. He's better off where he is. I haven't seen his chart but I talked to a nurse. He's had trouble breathing and is on intravenous fluids. There's no way we could help him here. Emergency supplies are being airlifted in and the Lions Gate Bridge may open tomorrow. That'll improve operations a lot. Tony needs full-time medical care. He needs doctors, nurses, and supplies I can't get."

He dried his hands on the towel that hung off the fridge door and I sensed he wasn't telling me everything he knew. I decided to stop asking questions, because maybe I wasn't ready for the answers. I stirred the pot a little slower and the creamy smell wafted up. "I made extra risotto so there'd be leftovers. You and I could take him some tonight."

Greg shook his head impatiently. "Rowan, have you heard anything I've been telling you? It's *dangerous* out there. They aren't letting anyone into the hospital who isn't seriously injured. There has been looting, assault, rape—whatever terrible things people are capable of—it's all happening. People are being attacked for very little."

I knew a scare tactic when I heard one, and resented him trying to manipulate me with fear. I guessed he didn't want me to see Tony because he knew he'd have to leave if Tony found out he was staying here. My temper flared but I stayed silent.

"Did Jake tell you what happened to his mother?"

"No. I'm not sure he knows." Not sure I care.

"Well, then." Greg sat at the table and laced his hands behind his head. "He might not know."

"Know what?" Michael came up from the basement, bleary eyed as usual. "Wow, that smells awesome. I'm guessing Jake won't mind eating this." He tried to take the wooden spoon but I jabbed it at him like a weapon. He went into the cupboard and brought out a jar of mixed nuts and dried fruit, took a handful and slid it over to Greg.

As if he heard his name, Jake shuffled into the kitchen. The rest of us stopped talking but he didn't seem to notice.

"Mom wants to eat with me on the front porch." He sniffed the risotto. "Smells good."

I watched him load a tray with two bowls, cutlery, and napkins, which he folded into roses. The paper flowers were beautiful. Perfect. They made me want to cry. Jake caught my eye and smiled as he picked up the tray. No one said anything until the screen door squeaked shut and we could hear their voices on the porch.

"Greg saw Tony and he's really sick." I spoke quietly.

Michael cut a look at Greg who nodded solemnly. Instead of telling us more about Tony, Greg changed the subject back to me. "I'm trying to discourage your sister from leaving the yard again."

"Why would she do that?" Michael's growl sounded exactly like Tony's.

I handed each of them a bowl and said, "I only wanted to take Tony some food so he wouldn't have to eat hospital crap. What's wrong with that?"

"And how're you going to get there?" Michael talked through a mush of rice and mushrooms.

"Same as before. It's only five K. I can jog that in no time." Five K was a warm up in hockey training. Besides I already proved I could get there and back without a problem. Well, without any problems Michael knew about. Besides Greg could take me if he wanted to.

"That's not was I was thinking and you know it." Michael shovelled in more risotto. "The army's moved in now and you'd probably get nabbed by one of the patrols."

"Exactly. You shouldn't even think about being out on the streets right now. That's my point," Greg said. Who voted him president? "Did you know that Linda had made it all the way over the Ironworkers' Bridge before she got into trouble? She had got herself a bike and was burning down the off-ramp. That was the day of the quake."

"But when she got here, it was the second morning," I said.

"Right. She had an accident and hit her head—she thinks. She's lucky to be here. While she was unconscious, someone stole her bike, jewellery, and purse. She remembers nothing more until the next day. It took her a while to figure out who she was and where she was headed. Eventually she crossed a busted pedestrian bridge to this side of the creek where lots of people were camping. One guy gave her water and trail mix. Then she got lost on one of the trails in the dark. After that her memory goes fuzzy. She remembers hitting her head again. She passed out and didn't wake until it was pitch dark out. She started walking toward what she hoped was north. She was almost all the way back to the park entrance when she realized she had walked the wrong way."

Greg folded his arms in front of him on the table. He gave me a stern look in case I wasn't getting the it's-dangerous-out-there message. "Linda walked back into that forest and found the steps to Arborlynn Drive but they were half destroyed. She climbed up them and thought once she had done that she would be home free. That was when things got worse. A cougar jumped her from behind but a couple out doing a neighbourhood patrol came in with pepper spray. They managed to spray the cat without getting her. They tried to get her to stay and accept first aid but she said, no, she had to get home and kept walking."

"She has no idea what time she got back here. She saw her house and all the wind went out of her. She woke up in the morning and she was sleeping under the back deck, the only part of the house still standing. You pretty much know what happened after that. I've been treating her for concussion plus some ugly cuts and bruises."

"So you're saying if I go to visit Tony, I'm going to be attacked by a mountain lion?"

"I'm saying you have no idea what the risks are out there. Cougars may be the least of your worries."

We dropped the conversation when the screen door creaked open. Linda came in and poured a glass of water. She went to the roster sheet on the fridge and struck through the last two hours of Jake's watch.

"Midnight is too late for Jacob to be up," she said. "I'll take the last hours of his shift. It'll give me time to draw up some chore sheets so we can get this house back in order."

Greg chuckled but Michael and I looked at each other, open-mouthed. The laundry was done. The kitchen was tidy, other than the spiders getting out of hand with their end-of-summer web-spinning but c'mon. We were in the middle of a disaster zone. Staring out at the world, keeping the garden alive, listening to the radio, and bracing ourselves for the next lot of crazies at the gate, those were our main activities now.

After dinner Michael and Greg settled down with Tony's big chessboard at the kitchen table. The radio played in the background and when it was announced that the twenty-four hour curfew had been cut to a 9:00 PM to 9:00 AM one, we all cheered. I didn't know why exactly, because we knew we had to stay in the compound until most people had food, water, and shelter again. Still it felt like the first thin wedge of freedom had come back into our lives.

I sat at the end of the table and watched them play for a bit. Mostly my mind drifted to Tony and how sick he was. "Trouble breathing" didn't sound good. When Linda went out to the porch for her shift and ordered Jake to bed, I followed him downstairs so he wouldn't feel so alone. Seeing Linda boss him around made me grateful that Tony wasn't there to do the same thing to me. I settled into my bedroom with the dog-eared copy of *Divergent* that Lexy had loaned me at the start of the summer. She'd be home in a week and I needed to start reading it. I heard Michael come down and head back to his room. I knew he'd put in his earplugs and be dead to the world until his alarm blasted a few minutes before his midnight shift. Even then Jake would wake up first and he'd have to shake Michael to get him up.

I couldn't stop thinking about Tony. I felt ashamed that I compared him to Linda. He wasn't nearly as controlling as she was and he was the only person I knew who was prepared for this disaster. I should have been thanking him, not resenting him.

I needed to try one more time, to see him and tell him how great his plans had been.

I wouldn't bring him down with stories about Michael's sprained ankle or Jake, Linda, and Greg moving in. Tony needed to think things were good inside the compound. Hearing that the house was solid and we were all getting along would make him get well faster.

If Greg understood how important it was that I see Tony, I knew he'd understand. I'd give him one more chance to help me. If he refused, I had Plan B: I'd go on my own.

Upstairs, Greg wasn't in the kitchen or the living room but the front door was open. I heard Greg and Linda on the front porch so I decided to join them and shadow Greg until I got him alone. A plastic chair groaned as someone sat in it. I was almost at the front door when Linda's voice reached me.

"What are you doing here, Ray? Jake thinks his father's dead. What am I supposed to tell him now?" She sounded waspish.

Holy. I bit my cheek to stop from gasping out loud. Greg was Jake's dad? His real name was Ray? I flattened myself against the hallway wall and listened.

Greg laughed softly. "Why do you have to tell him anything? It's not like I'm out here trying to fight you for custody."

Linda said, "That would be rich. You abandoned him even before he was born and then show up sixteen years later? Some judge is really going to listen to that. Still I'm surprised no one here has picked up on how alike you are. When you and Jake sit side-by-side, the resemblance is obvious."

"Have you said anything?"

"To who? Michael and Rowan? Not likely. What I want to know is how you found us."

"Your sister."

"She didn't."

"She did," Greg said. "She thinks we should get back together again."

"Lord save me from well-meaning relatives. Wendy promised she'd never tell, but she's always been a hopeless romantic. I can't tell you how many times she asked me if I wanted to find you. I always said the same thing. No. She must have been thrilled when you called her. She's never liked Phil—thinks he's too dull for me." She laughed, deep and humourless. "But why all this cloak and dagger stuff? A fake name? Why didn't you just phone me?"

"I was marking my time, getting ready. "I got to Vancouver a week ago and started watching your house, trying to get a better look at Jake, because I knew everything would change the minute I met him."

"You were stalking us?"

"That's an unpleasant word. Let's just say I didn't want to interrupt your life if there was any doubt. It wasn't until I followed him into the park and the earthquake hit that I saw him up close. There's no mistaking the Sewchuk eyes and face, is there? Anyway, you should be grateful that I was around when the quake hit. When I got to Jake, he was disorientated. His friends were pretty clueless about what to do and I think they all felt better with me there."

Clueless? We were already treating him for shock before Greg showed up.

"Let's see...hm...the last time I saw you was Boxing Day 1997. I cooked dinner. You ate it. Then you went out for cigarettes despite the fact that I'd asked you to stop smoking because I was pregnant. Sound right so far?"

Greg murmured something but Linda kept the talking stick. "Then you cleaned out our bank account. The January rent cheque bounced. I had to go on welfare until Jacob was born. Just those few months though. I took two jobs and parked Jacob with whoever would take him while I worked twelve hours a day. All that time, not so much as a phone call from you."

She stopped talking as if she expected him to say something. He didn't.

"Finally we moved to a tiny basement suite where my view of the world was people's feet walking past. My landlady loved kids and babysat him for almost nothing while I worked and studied."

I wished I had a pen and paper. Jake couldn't find this stuff on Google.

Linda continued, "I finished my degree, got a job and searched for a decent man who'd take on a woman with student loans and a kid. I chose carefully. Sure Phil may not be much to look at but he's been a real father to Jacob, since the first day he met him. He makes good money—really good— and he's generous with it. Wendy calls it a *mariage d'intérêt* but I've got deep affection for Phil, to say nothing of a deep loyalty. He doesn't deserve to lose his son to you and I won't let that happen."

I tucked the expression *mariage d'intérêt* away at the back of my brain and forced myself to keep listening.

"We've had to move around a bit, even live overseas a few years because of his work, but now we're settled in North Vancouver, leading an ordinary suburban life. I don't want that life disturbed. Understood?"

Greg's answer was inaudible. A mosquito landed on my bare thigh. I felt the sting and watched it feast on my blood. I didn't dare move. Secrets about Jake and Greg wrestled in my brain. Should I tell Jake? If it were me, I'd want to know. That was a push for *tell* him. Linda lied to Jake his entire life, like his father was some sort of dirty secret. Another push for *tell*. But if I told him about Greg, he might hate me for knowing before he did. Or he might retreat into silence and I knew how lonely that world was. Smackdown on that idea.

"So what have you been up to?" Linda asked after a long pause. Her tone was sarcastic-friendly.

"I never married. I shacked up a couple of times. I burned bridges with almost every woman I ever cared about. I've written you a hundred letters of apology but I always tore them up. It wasn't all my fault you know."

It was his turn to wait for an answer that didn't come.

"Hell, you knew that I was terrified of being a father. I was only nineteen and it felt like you were putting a noose around my neck. You said you were taking care of contraception but instead you trapped me. I shouldn't have trusted you either."

I wished I could see their faces. Greg sounded bitter. Linda sounded angry.

He coughed a couple of times. "But I did do one thing to make amends; I saved part of every paycheque that I ever got after I left you. And I have that money still, for Jake's education, or for whatever Jake wants to do with it. Over thirty thousand dollars."

The plastic chair scraped. Linda uttered a tiny, "Oh."

I thought about Jake and how his mother controlled him. I wondered if she would even tell Jake that the money came from his biological father. Probably not. Maybe I had to tell Jake, just in case Linda forgot, accidentally-on-purpose.

Linda spoke again. "Well, well. Sixteen years later and you deliver. For Jacob's sake I'm glad. But we'll wait until Phil is home before Jacob hears a word of this."

Information was power, something Jake had very little of. Maybe he needed to know now.

"Why do you do that? Call him Jacob when his friends call him Jake?"

"Friends? Those trashy kids from here? They're not his friends and they're sure not a yardstick of how my son should be addressed. I think the sooner I'm strong enough to take over the running of this house, the sooner we'll see some real order here. These teenagers need some rules laid down for them."

Blood pounded in my ears. How dare she talk about Michael and me that way! How dare she plan to take over our house! I waited to hear Greg defend us.

"You're wrong. Rowan and Michael are fine kids."

"I knew it. You've got the hots for that girl. She's sure got her eyes on you."

I flushed with embarrassment. What was she talking about? Why was she trying to make me sound ridiculous?

Greg's said icily, "Don't you think she's a bit young for me? Besides, she's just confused in that clingy, adolescent way."

A humiliated blush burned up my neck. I should never have dared to hope that anyone like Greg would treat me like an adult. No one did. Pure white hatred of the world at large spiked through me. I reminded myself to breathe as I crept back into the living room where Greg was camped out. His sleeping bag was thrown over the sofa and he'd emptied his pockets on to the end table. I ignored the wallet and reached for the bright orange lanyard with the paramedic ID on the end. He always wore the ID part tucked inside his shirt. In the half-light coming in from the porch I could read his real name plainly. *Ray Sewchuk.*

Well, if Greg or Ray, or whoever he really was, refused to help me get in to see Tony, I'd just have to help myself.

Greg didn't even like me. That was obvious now. Tony was right. Family were the only people who counted, the only people I could trust. My family needed to reconnect, for strength and unity and all that other Three Musketeer stuff that Tony was always spouting. Greg checked on Tony and now we knew for certain that he wasn't coming home soon. Michael was sleeping all the time. He wasn't acting like a commanding officer. He needed to know that Tony was coming home soon to get us working together again. The plain truth was I wanted to see Tony. I wanted to feel his protection again. I never thought I'd miss him so much.

CHAPTER 24 | ROWAN'S WAY

NORTH VANCOUVER

Greg's comments stung me all night long, as if he'd deliberately cheated Michael and me somehow. He lied about his name because he wanted to get closer to Jake and he didn't know how much Jake knew about him. That didn't give him a right to criticize Michael or me. The next morning my watch started at 7 AM but I rolled out of bed at six.

"Woke up and couldn't get back to sleep," I said to Michael who was slouched in the rocking chair.

He peered at me from under heavy-lidded eyes. "That's good because I keep nodding off." He seemed tired, like he had every day since the quake. He pushed himself out of the chair stiffly as if he were a million years old. Then he limped into the kitchen and made his usual before bed sandwich.

He ate it in a couple of mouthfuls and I hung around the top of the stairs and listened. When I heard his bedroom door close, I went to the kitchen and stuffed my backpack full of food for Tony. I hung Greg's ID inside my T-shirt. Greg. He put the putrid taste of humiliation in my mouth but I'd replace it with a sense of achievement. I'd see Tony and I'd help him. And I'd bring news that would snap Michael out of his lethargy. Morgans looked after each other.

I swept my hair off my shoulders into a ponytail and put on the silver St. Sebastian's medal that Lexy gave me at the start of hockey finals last year. Then I sat on the porch rocking and waiting for the sun to rise and brighten the road a bit. I tried to not think about Tony's temper when I arrived at the hospital against his orders.

I didn't want to think about Greg's words any longer. I wished they would die. Instead they repeated in my head in an infinite loop. How had I been so wrong about him? He had used me to stay close to Jake. I stood up abruptly and the rocker tipped forward. I was stupider than stupid. I had to get away.

I heaved up my pack and took a long drink. As I set the bottle down on the table beside the rocker, I jumped. Jake stood in the doorway. He wore Greg's paramedic hoodie and navy shorts. I hadn't noticed how muscular his legs were before.

"Do you play soccer?" I asked, trying not to stare.

He bit into an apple and talked as he chewed. "Not allowed. I do a lot of Pilates and work out in our home gym."

The sweet juicy smell of the apple reminded me I hadn't eaten breakfast. I glanced at Jake again. Something about him had changed in the past few days. He spoke in full sentences. He met my eyes as he talked. He stood a little taller. Now I knew to look for it, I could see Greg in him. Same hair. Same mouth. Same height.

I fingered the strap on my pack. First thought—run for it and hope that Jake didn't sound the alarm. Then I thought I should I stay and set him straight about how his father was alive, how his father was someone he knew and liked. But I remembered the way Greg criticized Michael and me and I didn't want to say his name out loud.

He nodded at my pack. "Where're you going?"

"That's my business."

"But it's your watch isn't it?"

"So? It's daytime and the house is full of people. I don't think anyone is going to try anything now."

"I could cover for you if you like." A wide, eager smile transformed his face. He was almost handsome. "I'll tell everyone that you're sick. We could put a do not disturb sign on your bedroom door."

"Do you mind?" I smiled back at him.

"No, I like early mornings. They always smell like hope."

Just when I thought Jake wasn't so different after all, a comment like that slipped out. He was one weird dude. I tightened the waist strap on my pack and tried to think of an answer.

"How're you getting out?" Jake said. "Greg's special exit?"

"What do you know about that?"

"I got tired of waiting yesterday afternoon so I checked out what you and Greg were doing."

"You spied on us?"

"Just made sure you guys weren't in trouble."

"Good. Glad you were paying attention." I juggled my water bottle from hand to hand. "Yeah it was my plan to go out the back way."

"Brilliant," he said. I listened hard for any tone of sarcasm but heard only kindness and encouragement.

"Thanks," I said, walking to the kitchen. Suddenly I felt self-conscious at the way he looked at me. I took out a notepad and printed "Do Not Disturb" across the top page. As I threw the pad back in the drawer and picked up the travel chess game and in case Tony could find someone to play with. I slid it into the cargo pocket of my jeans. As an afterthought, I clipped the bear spray to my belt.

Waving goodbye, I bolted from the house before Jake could change his mind. I walked fast and minutes later wound my way along back lanes and pedestrian paths. I listened for the sound of mechanical noises like police cars or army jeeps. I sniffed the morning air, wondering what hope smelled like. At first I only caught the acrid scent of fire but then, underneath it, the reassuring aroma of coffee from someone's camping kitchen. Knowing that some people had shelter and a stove for cooking encouraged me. One block of houses looked like they'd been randomly torched with a flamethrower. Some buildings still smouldered. I kept to the middle of the shattered lane, in case people lurked behind the dark hedges and crippled fences, waiting for a girl with a heavy backpack of food. The windowless houses gave this area a soulless air, as if their eyes had been poked out by a giant's fingers.

Coming down St. George's I saw a row of ambulances parked outside the ER entrance. Paramedics unloaded a patient on a stretcher. My heart lifted. If the ambulances were bringing people back to the hospital, then things must be getting better. The barricades were still up but only a few soldiers patrolled the grounds. The crowds on the outside side of the barricades had thinned, but there were still a hundred people or more sitting at camping tables, playing cards, waiting to see family and friends inside. Not everyone had a paramedic's ID to get them past the guard dogs.

The soldiers paid no attention to the crowds. One female soldier wore earbuds and marched, dancelike, in time to her tunes. Her head bobbed and she half smiled as she moved. The inside of the barricades seemed kind of friendly compared to the first day after the quake. I skipped toward the hospital; I'd think of something to say when I got there. A closer look showed that the person on the stretcher had one arm wrapped in bandages. It stopped just below the elbow. The face was burned and one eye was patched. The bandages looked like a Halloween costume. I turned away so the person underneath all the wrapping couldn't see my horror.

A large family group advanced on the two soldiers standing sentry in front of the entrance. There were four women, one with a bruised face and bloody arm with a bone poking out, a man, a teenage boy and a little girl. They talked in rapid Farsi, all at the same time.

A woman near me stopped her game of Solitaire, glanced at them, then at me, and back at the Iranian family again. The extended family had reached the soldiers and one of the women stepped forward as spokesperson. In perfect English she pointed to the bleeding one.

"My sister needs a doctor," she said.

The soldiers spoke quietly and I guessed they told her about the "one patient, one carer rule." The man stepped forward and took the woman's arm as if he wanted to go into the hospital with her. The first woman said no, she had to go in with the injured one. The soldiers looked irritated and the family looked determined. I fingered Greg's paramedic pass, picking my moment.

One of the other women translated quickly to the bleeding one, pointed to the hospital and to the man. The injured woman clung to the first woman and held her arm tight, and began screaming in English, "Don't leave me. Don't leave me!"

The fourth woman prostrated herself in front of the soldiers, her hands twisted upward. "Please, let me go with her also. Her English is poor and her husband doesn't speak any English at all."

The woman soldier yanked out her earbuds and started talking at the same time as her male counterpart. The family argued back, in two different languages. Right on cue the little girl burst into noisy tears and started begging too. The teen-aged boy yelled and shook his fist at the soldiers. I marched forward with a big show of confidence. Covering the photo on the paramedic ID with my thumb, I flashed it at the guard who barely noticed me. That's the good thing about being tall: people always think you're older than you are.

Inside I picked my way over the filthy and injured people who sat on every inch of chair and floor space in the waiting area, wall-to-wall people who hadn't had the chance to wash, let alone shower, for five days. Scents of sweat and blood singed the back of my nose. People moaned. Some argued and snapped at their neighbours like bad-tempered dogs on short leashes.

At the reception desk a man in a tight blue turban rested his head on his folded arms. I stood in front of him and cleared my throat for a minute. It took me a while to figure out that he was asleep. If the wailing of all the desperate people didn't wake him, I knew I wouldn't either. I stepped around to the computer terminal and flicked the mouse to wake it up. I typed "Morgan Anthony Earl" into the name boxes. Bingo. 410A.

I ducked down the nearest hallway. Seeing an open linen locker, I grabbed a set of scrubs. I strode briskly away, hoping no one had seen me. In a washroom I pulled the scrubs over my clothes. Way too short and way too wide. I used the belt from my jeans to stop the pale aqua pants from falling down. The top hung loose and hid my belt. I checked for official staff before stepping into the hallway again. None. Just sick and injured people everywhere. I flung my backpack over my shoulder and ran up the stairs to the fourth floor.

The heat hit me first. This floor cooked in the rising heat from the three floors below it. The clinging smell of industrial cleaners didn't completely mask the darker traces of human misery. I fought the urge to turn and run. At the far end of the hall a janitor mopped around a kid who was sleeping on the floor with his head in his mother's lap.

People lined the hallway, some sitting on the ground, the others lying on cots. I focused on my shoes and tried to be deaf to the cries of pain and helplessness. 410A was the only room with a closed door. I checked the number twice and peeked through the small window. Five patients were pushed into a space designed for two. Everyone appeared to be sleeping. I tiptoed inside. It smelled worse than the hallway. A rancid odour tainted the air, a stench that clawed down my throat to my stomach. I gagged and clamped my hand over my nose and mouth. *Couldn't they keep this place cleaner?*

On the beds and gurneys lay a silver-haired woman, a dark-skinned man, an old man, and a young boy. There, nearest the window with his face turned away, lay Tony. I walked to his side quietly. His face was sunken. I'd never seen him with a beard before and the few days' growth made him look ancient. I put my pack down and leaned in close.

"Tony?" I said quietly.

He didn't answer.

"I brought you some food." A little louder.

"Tony?" Loud this time, but he still didn't answer.

"I've got risotto. And espresso just the way you like it." Next to him the silver-haired woman lay on her back, staring at the ceiling. My eyes darted to the next patient. The dark-skinned man was on his side, arms sprawling out of the bed in front of him. He stared wide-eyed without blinking.

A hiccup of despair slipped out.

"Tony." I touched his shoulder. Through the thin hospital gown, his skin felt cold. I stepped back and shook my head. I closed my eyes tight as if I was a frightened kid. I prayed when I opened them again that Tony would wake up. He'd look at me in rage and yell so loud that people would come running and someone would turn me over to the police. As long as I didn't look, it wasn't real but the stink in the room made me open my eyes again. There was no hope in this smell. It was the smell of death, of bodies rotting and organs decaying. I refused to believe it.

"Please no. Daddy, wake up! It's Rowan here and I need you. Please talk to me."

I climbed on the narrow bed beside him and wrapped my arms around his stiff body. He was so cold and I tried to warm him. My heart stopped beating for a minute. "Daddy, Daddy, Daddy."

I touched his left arm but snapped my hand quickly away from the dressing over his wound. The gauze was stiff with yellow muck, as if it hadn't been changed for days. Could that happen? Could he have been forgotten somehow? I thought of the hundreds of people waiting in the other rooms, in the hallways, behind the barricades outside and knew the worst had happened.

No. It couldn't be true. It mustn't be true. Only a week ago, in the early hours of the morning of the earthquake, Tony dragged Michael and me out of bed. He made us look at Jupiter near the waning moon. He swept his arm across the sky and said we weren't seeing stars, we were seeing the openings in heaven where our grandparents were shining down on us, letting know they were happy. Usually so practical, he became a different person when he took out his telescope. The night skies transformed him into a kinder man, full of dreams and passion. He'd been making me join him for special celestial events since I could remember. So that night I took a quick look through the telescope, grumbled the way I always did, and went back to bed. I never appreciated how much of himself he was showing me on those clear sky nights. I never said thank you. Now I never could.

Then it hit me. I was holding a corpse. I scrambled to the floor but my knees wobbled. I stopped breathing, bent double, and retched over the garbage can.

Morgans don't cry, Tony always said. Tears flooded down my cheeks and snot ran down my face as I stood in that hideous death room. I didn't hear the door open.

"You shouldn't be in here," said a male voice, low and grim.

Two attendants in green hospital uniforms pushed a long flat cart, stacked with body bags. They wore rubber gloves and face masks.

"No," I yelled, standing in front of Tony's body. "You can't have him. He's my dad. He's coming home with me." I pushed the words out and my throat clamped shut. Before I could speak again I had to swallow a few mouthfuls of the fetid air. "He always said he'd die in his own home."

He needed to be buried there, inside the walls of Fortress Tony, inside the place he felt strongest. The bigger orderly turned tired eyes to me and pushed his long, grey hair behind his ears. Then he unzipped a body bag and moved to where the kid was.

"Give us a minute, Ken," the other person said, and dragged her mask down. Yes, her voice was female and I had to look twice. With ropey muscular arms, she could have been a hockey player and that comforted me. She rested against the windowsill. "My name's Sydney. Call me Syd. Who're you?" She folded her hands together and studied them. She might have been praying.

"Rowan Morgan," I sobbed, "and this is my dad. Or it was." Pain burst through me like boiling oil. I trembled with the effort of not crying again.

"Rowan. That's a strong name for a strong girl. And you have to be very strong right now, don't you?" She wheezed at the end of each sentence, a short intake of breath. "And you can be strong, can't you? For your dad?" She reached the shelf beside Tony's bed and yanked out a wad of tissues and handed them to me. She smiled, soft and kindly. For a minute she felt like a friend.

"When did he die?" I blew my nose three times. My eyes burned, sandy and raw.

She picked up Tony's chart. "Early this morning, just after midnight actually."

If I'd come last night instead of letting Greg talk me out of it, I could have said goodbye.

"Where're you taking him?" I bit my lip. If Syd showed me any sympathy I would burst into tears again. Time to put on my warrior mask. I dug out my phone and took a couple of pictures. I didn't know whether I was being desperate or ghoulish but I wanted to remember.

"Down to the morgue."

"When was someone going to tell us that he'd died?" My tongue seemed to have swollen and speaking got really, really hard. I glanced over to where Ken perched beside the kid, a body bag loose in his hands. His head nodded and even though he sat upright, it looked like he was sleeping.

Syd touched my shoulder and her gentle brown eyes met mine. "Right now it's all hands on the pump and we're all kind of exhausted around here. When the phone lines are up, they'll find someone with the time to phone next of kin but right now it's kind of impossible. We're just trying to keep a list of who we've processed."

Processed.

She smiled sadly, as if she was too tired to find a nicer word. She handed me the gym bag at the end of the bed. "You should take your father's things."

I snatched the bag from her and opened it. Everything was there: his razor, his pyjamas, *The Worst-Case Scenario Survival Handbook.* I froze. I didn't know what to do.

Syd watched me silently until Ken came to life at the other end of the room and said, "We'd better get to it. There's four more down the hall we have to pick up."

"Yeah, right," she said and gave me one last look. "Before you go, would you mind leaving those scrubs here? Laundry's a bit of an issue right now."

I had no reason to refuse, no reason to do anything except go home and hide. I stripped off the scrubs and threw them on the bed. Then I picked up my pack. Heavy.

"Do you want some food?" I asked. "Ken? What about you?" I dumped out the container of risotto, the thermos of coffee, the cookies, fruit and salad.

Syd's face shone with *yes.* Ken came over and the two of them jammed as much as they could into their pockets.

Ken said, "We'll come back for the rest," and put the thermos and plastic containers into an empty patient locker.

Tony's stuff weighed nothing compared to the food I'd just ditched. Yet somehow it felt a hundred times heavier. I tried his gold RCMP ring on each of my fingers. The only place it didn't slide and turn was on my thumb. I would wear it forever. More tears scalded my eyes.

I looked at Tony one last time before I headed for the stairs. I felt older than dirt.

CHAPTER 25
SURVIVAL

NORTH VANCOUVER

Right until the moment I weaseled my way into the hospital, I thought everything was going to get better. It might take a very long time but eventually things would be the way they were before. Now I knew that was impossible. The last tatters of my old life had been ripped away. Tony had been gone for almost a week and I had waited for him to come home. He wasn't going to.

I trudged away from the hospital barely registering the stares of other people who waited to get inside. As I slipped through the barricade, the Solitaire woman looked up from her cards and shouted, "How come she got in, if we've got to stay out?"

The Iranian family, missing two of the women, pushed toward the barricade. In a second, everyone who had been waiting so patiently, flanked around them. Bodies pressed forward and I swam upstream against them. Grief stripped away my manners. I used my elbows to push people away and didn't care when someone screeched after I stepped on a bare foot. That was the last sound I heard as silence descended over me and I closed out the rest of the world.

Thoughts and memories of Tony cartwheeled through my brain. The last time I saw him we fought. The same way we had been fighting almost non-stop for the past year. Lately it was about the motorcycle I'd wanted to buy. The green Kawasaki. A bleat of morbid laughter escaped me when I thought about the battle we'd been having at least once a week. In the worst moments, an evil part of me wished he was dead. Now he was and somehow it seemed to be all my fault. Why wasn't I nicer to him that last afternoon? He'd been out searching for us, and he was worried.

If I had a motorcycle now I'd jump on it and ride. I leaned against a crooked telephone phone and closed my eyes. I imagined my right hand, opening the throttle, my left hand flicking the clutch as I changed gears. The green Ninja flew up the road. I wouldn't stop until I got somewhere that the earthquake hadn't touched. I'd ride until I found a landscape where trees stood straight and houses had power and water.

When I broke out of my dream, I was still surrounded by battered homes. I forced myself forward and skirted the public campgrounds. I looked like just another homeless person on the street, drifting from nowhere to nowhere. My pack was thin and flat now. No one would attack me for its contents.

The rattle of the chess set in my pocket made me think of Michael. Michael—what would I tell him?

The people camping on Grand Boulevard seemed to be having a party. Some were laughing. A volunteer in an orange T-shirt led a group of small kids in nonsense songs. *I'm a little teapot.* Children giggled. Their singing and laughter reached me from far away, like the end of a long train tunnel.

I would never see Tony again. All the memories I had of him were all I'd ever have. He wouldn't be there for my high school graduation. If I went to university he'd never know. He'd never be grandfather to my babies. That didn't feel true. It didn't feel possible. I floated along, lost in some faraway place.

Voices and sounds echoed around me but they meant nothing. Without warning tears boiled over again, running down into my mouth. I cried until it felt like a blood vessel in my head was going to burst and I might pass out.

I slid my shaking hand into my pocket for a Kleenex and found Tony's cell. Turning it on, I found unsent text messages stuck in the dead zone of no service. One to me and one to Michael on the day of the quake. Two more when he was in the hospital. They both said the same thing and a vise-grip crushed my chest. *Love you kids. Take care of each other.*

There was another one just to me and it read: *Don't ride faster than your angel can fly.* Goosebumps popped up on my arms when I realized what the words meant. While giving me the blessing to get my bike, he was telling to make good choices. He knew I was going to fly free of him.

It made me think of when I was first learning to skate and how I used to sprint into his arms at the end of the lesson. He'd laugh and say, "My little girl is growing up." Sometimes he added, "Don't grow up too fast my little Rowanberry."

Maybe that's what our fight was really about. Maybe he was just sad that I was starting to do grown-up things now, that I couldn't be his little girl any more. Maybe he wondered where his loving daughter Rowan had gone, just like I wondered who had taken my father and left a grouch in his place. Why did we waste our last hours fighting? I hoped he forgave me before he died.

I followed the roads blindly until I came to the path in the woods behind Tony's house. In the midday heat, the forest smelled like baking berry pie. I pushed my way through thickets and climbed over fallen trees. Tears blurred my vision. A grey streak shot in front of me. *Misty.* I dropped to one knee.

"Hey kitty. C'mere." My voice came out high and rusty, as if I hadn't used it for a year. Misty stopped on the side of the dried out creek and kneaded the dead leaves. I murmured her name over and over, like a lullaby. Something moved on the edge of my vision. Jake. With the cat carrier! I held up my hand up and he stopped. I knelt on the ground and waited. From the general area of our house I became aware of a low rumble. I tried to read Jake's face and what I saw there wasn't good. He chewed his gum hard and fast. When I stopped watching Misty for a second, she disappeared and the leaves of salal thicket shivered behind her. I squinted but saw nothing so I stood and stretched my calf muscles. No second chances for her. I prayed she'd come back when she was hungry, but I couldn't wait. I turned toward the house.

"How'd she get out?"

"Mom went into your room."

"Yeah?"

"Misty ran out the door before we could stop her."

"What was your mom doing in my room?" I tried to keep the anger out of my voice.

"She said if I had to do your shift then you could do mine. When she knocked on your door and you didn't answer, she went in anyway."

I jerked my head toward the street. "What's the commotion?"

"Greg had to go to the hospital so Mom did his watch. Then those neighbours, the ones two houses away—"

"The Redgraves? The ones with the four obnoxious boys?"

"Yeah them. They came over and she let them in." Jake kicked a rock into the salal bushes.

"Where the hell was Michael?"

"He was sleeping—with ear plugs in. By the time I woke him up, the Redgraves were already in the basement. Mom gave them a couple of cases of canned food, preserves, meat from the freezer, and some of the bottled water."

"God, why would she do that?"

She and Mrs. Redgrave are in the same book club. She said all the mothers have to stick together."

"How did she know about all the food and water supplies?" I didn't think she'd ever even been down to the basement.

Even in the shade I saw a flush crawl over Jake's face. A pungent smell of sweat wafted off him. "I…I'm sorry. I was trying to make her feel better. I told how well stocked the house was."

I stood, my mouth bone dry, and searched for words that wouldn't blow him backwards. It was my fault. I'd used Tony's supplies to reassure him exactly the same way. He had copied my example.

He smiled slightly. "She did one thing you'll like."

"Yeah?"

"She gave the Redgraves every ounce of alcohol she could find."

I shook my head. "The lock to the cellar?"

"They pried it open."

"So what's all that noise?" As if I didn't know.

"The Redgraves told others. There're some people at the front gate asking for food." He shoved his hands deep in his pockets.

"Where's your mom?"

"On the front porch. With Michael. They're fighting. She wants to give more away, look after more people. He's telling her that the more we give away, the more people will hear about it and it won't stop until everything's gone."

"Forget Misty. Michael needs us." I fought my way through the thorny barberry and blackberry bushes that protected the back fence, the way to Greg's secret passage. The stopgap gate yawned open and anyone could have got in. I resisted telling Jake how careless that was as I squeezed into the back yard. After he followed, I closed the gate and snapped the lock shut behind us. He avoided my eyes and I felt mean. It wasn't his fault that this mother wanted to rule the world. The bitterness of her betrayal winded me like a punch to the stomach.

"Mom only meant to help," Jake said without much conviction.

I spat out the first sour thought in my head. "Your mom makes a lot of decisions for others that aren't hers to make. You should know that."

Jake caught up to me on the back deck. "What do you mean?" His hand clawed my shoulder and he spun me around to face him.

"Why don't you ask her who your father is? Your real, live father." My ragged breaths took in the smell of him, sweat and body wash.

"My father's dead."

"Is he really? Who told you that?"

His jaw tightened. He let go of me and ran out to the front porch. By the time I got there he was standing between Michael and his mother.

"What sort of question is that?" Linda asked, hands on her hips.

"Is. My. Real. Father. Dead?" He clipped the words as is if she were hard of hearing.

"Don't be ridiculous. You know he is." Linda smoothed the sides of her purple capris with the palms of her hands.

"I don't believe you," Jake said.

"Not now Jacob," she half whispered. Taking a deep breath, she moved toward him as if she was going to put her arm around his shoulders like she usually did.

He pushed her away. "Tell me."

The crowd at the gate was getting noisier. Michael went to the top of the stairs, and glared at the thirty or forty people who stood a cautious distance away from the fence. He looked alone, vulnerable, and my chest tightened.

"Go home," he shouted. His voice sounded worn out, exhausted.

Behind us Linda was trying to deflect Jake. "We'll talk tonight, after dinner. Right now we have to help Michael."

"No," Jake said, spit flying.

As if they thought Jake was speaking to them, the people outside chanted louder, "Food, water! Food, water! Food, water!"

Linda said, "Later," in a final tone of voice that I recognized from arguments with Tony. She trotted down to the fence and talked to the mob, gesturing wildly as if she was trying to semaphore them into calmness. I wondered if she was promising them more food later or asking them to leave. Either way it didn't matter. No one was paying attention.

I squeezed Jake's hand. "Later," I said, my way of promising to tell him if Linda didn't.

He nodded and his fingers wrapped around mine, warm and strong. I gave his hand one last squeeze and strode to Michael's side.

"I'm going to get the heavy artillery," I whispered.

Something deep inside me, something primal, had woken. My pulse pounded in my ears and I flew downstairs. I'd made a decision and no one could stop me. Our house would be defended at all costs.

The coolness of the basement rushed over me, perfumed lightly by Michael's woody shampoo. The noise out front dulled to distant hum as I stood in front of the cupboard that hid the gun safe and focused. My bones were lengthening and my skin was stretching. I was smashing out of the mould that had strangled me all summer. This was it, my leap into a new life. I'd take the guns and disperse the crowd with a few economical rounds of ammunition. That was exactly what Tony would tell me to do if he were here.

He said the guns were there to protect us in case of a major disaster. A scene rose clearly in my head. The crowd would be scared, stunned and voiceless for a minute. Then they'd turn away and go home, leaving us alone forever. Yes, that's what Tony wanted me to do. For once this summer I'd do what he wanted.

I pulled open the wall to the gun safe and touched the icy combination dial with my fingertips. Slowly I spun the numbers and when the cylinders released, I flipped the handle open. Inside stood three cases: two rigid plastic rifle cases and a leather shotgun case. The shotgun would give the biggest bang for the buck. I imagined racking the slide, hearing the mechanical *shuck* that announced the ammunition was loaded and ready to fire. I reached for the brown case and as my fingers brushed the thick leather handle, it zapped me like an electrical shock.

Stop. Think. Observe. Plan.

What did I really know about guns? Not much. A few afternoons on the shooting range. No recent experience. Tony was the firearms expert in our family. The memory of his cold body descended around me, a wall of ice. One of these guns had killed him. When he opened this safe a week ago, all he planned to do was put a deer out of its misery. All his years of training and lectures about the safe handling and storage of firearms failed to protect him.

I yanked my hand back and thought of the rising panic in the desperate faces outside. One simple mistake might create another tragedy. It could stain Tony's land with unnecessary bloodshed. That blood would be on my hands.

Weapons can escalate conflict.

The thought sailed up from deep inside me, not from Tony, not from Mom, but from my own understanding of what I faced. I imagined how the appearance of guns might make the frantic crowd even crazier. People might see our guns as an answer to other problems and be twice as determined to get inside, to get their hands on our weapons, maybe even use them against us.

As I wrung my hands and stared at the guns, the last of my conviction drained from my body. Standing in front of me were two options: arm myself, as Tony intended, and hope for the best. Or I could make my own decision: close the safe and pray that the electrified fence was enough to keep the hordes at bay.

How many gun accidents were too many? One. And it had already happened.

Tony's choice had been fatal and I would learn from that. I'd find another way, a different plan, and we'd save the compound without the risk of deadly force. Nothing was worth protecting no matter what the costs.

I stretched the ache out of my skin and bones, and felt taller and less afraid than I had seconds before as I reached for the gun. With new confidence, I rummaged through the safe, searching for anything that might be useful. On the top shelf were boxes of ammunition, enough to take out every single person in that crowd. I shuddered. On the shelf below that Tony's leather passport case lay on top of a few thick envelopes and an old wallet. I picked up the wallet and fanned through masses of twenty- and fifty-dollar bills. If the stores ever opened again we'd be able to buy everything we needed with this much cash. I grabbed out a handful of bills and folded them into my pocket. Maybe crazy people could be bought off. I locked the safe, closed the false wall and pushed cartons of old clothing in front of the cupboard.

Then I balled my hands and pounded them against my thighs. What could I use to shock and awe the crowd? I remembered a plastic storage tub, tucked inside Tony's fishing boat. I crept into the garage and tore the tarp off the boat. There it was, a waterproof container. I dug out one rocket and one handheld flare and charged back through the house to the front porch. Linda was sitting in the rocking chair, not looking at anyone in particular. Jake and Michael stood like two sentries on either side of the porch. I took a position between them.

"Go back to your homes and shelters now, please," I said in a firm voice.

"We're not going anywhere until you give us something," a thin man in torn overalls said. "We heard you've got enough food for a thousand people."

"You heard wrong," I lied. If they were certain of our supplies, they'd never go away. "Our shelves are empty. Our neighbours the Redgraves made sure of that today."

"They said you've got a supermarket in your basement," the man said and picked up a big rock and threw it over the fence. It thudded on the hood of Tony's truck and I could see the dent from where I stood. I remembered Tony slapping the driver's door just before he left. I flinched. He would never do that again.

Without another thought I lifted the rocket flare and aimed at the sky. Like an amateur, I closed my eyes and popped the pin. The flare banged as loud as a cannon and launched a thousand feet into the sky. Instantly the crowd shut up. People jumped. A couple ducked. Stunned faces looked up at me from the street. Some people ran away. I searched the thinning crowd but I couldn't see the Green Death guys at all. I hoped they had moved on, after easier pickings.

I popped the top on the handheld flare and it burst into flames, 15,000 candlepower of burning light. I trotted down to the fence and marched along wielding it at the strangers. Even from four feet away they felt its heat. People moved back, turned away from our house. The crowd thinned to a dozen determined campaigners but the mob power was gone.

When I got back to the porch Jake said, "That was awesome." He and Michael laughed nervously as if I had just grown horns.

"What've you done?" The rocker pitched noisily as Linda rose to her feet.

"What have I done? Ha. I wouldn't have had to do anything if it wasn't for you." I tried to bite back my frustration. Infighting wouldn't help anything. "You let people into the compound. You gave away our food—not yours—ours. My family's food."

She actually listened to me and, for a nanosecond, her face softened in apology. I took a deep breath. "Look we're all pretty stressed right now and probably we need to chill for a bit."

She lifted her chin and her face paled. Two trucks sped down the street toward us. They screeched to a halt outside the fence. Green Death gang members climbed out of the van and down from the back of the pickup, like spiders emptying a nest. I counted quickly, nine or ten, all guys. I hadn't seen that many together before. Two of them waved small hand tools in the air.

"You know what these are, kids?" Scarface held his aloft and grinned.

"Insulated wire cutters," Michael said as if he was announcing the weather. "Now what do we do?"

No one answered. I thought about the flares in the garage. A couple dozen maybe. Each one would burn about a minute. That might buy us half an hour—then what? We didn't have enough bear spray for crowd control. There were hunting, fishing, and kitchen knives, for all the good they would do. Green Death members were used to street fighting. We'd last about two seconds if we tried to take them on with handheld weapons.

So Michael, Linda, Jake and I stood transfixed for the few minutes it took to cut a large, gaping hole in the perimeter fence. Scarface and a guy in a muscle shirt and skinny jeans peeled back the chain-link as easy as a banana skin. They were coming in now no matter what we did.

The crowd on the street had formed again pushed towards the new entry gate like a single seething animal. Don Redgrave was the first one through the portal. He led the gang around the back of the house. They didn't bother with the kitchen; they were going straight to the cellar, to the mother lode.

I turned to go into the house, to lock the heavy security doors that isolated the living areas from the storage space.

Before I took my second step through the front door, Linda gasped, "Molotov cocktails!"

NORTH VANCOUVER

A couple of wiry dudes got out of the back of the van with arms full of glass bottles. Telltale wicks hung out of them. The bottles jostled and clinked as they walked closer. One guy dug a lighter out of his pocket.

"We're screwed," Michael said and sank down onto the plastic loveseat.

"No we're not." I shook his arm and tried to drag him to his feet. "We have to try to save this place. Please." His biceps felt rock hard under my fingers and I knew the two of us were physically strong enough to fight what was coming. "There's the big extinguisher in Tony's office. I'll get the one from the kitchen plus all the ones you made! C'mon. This is the best place on earth. We have to protect it."

He chewed his thumbnail and watched as the first firebomb was lit. I shook him one last time. "Michael," I screamed. "Fire extinguishers!"

"I'll get the hoses," Jake yelled.

"No! No water—water feeds gas fires!" I called. "Follow me."

Behind us I heard Michael pound into Tony's office. I sprinted to the kitchen and ripped open the door to the pantry. There on the floor was the box of homemade fire extinguishers that Michael had been assembling on his shifts. Shoving the box at Jake with my foot, I tore the fire blanket off the wall and grabbed the commercial extinguisher.

Before we got back to the living room, a window shattered. We arrived there just as Michael attacked with the big extinguisher. "Get low, into the vapour layer," he said from a deep knee bend.

Another missile followed. I'd never seen a Molotov cocktail before and it stupefied me. One second a fiery flare was airborne, then it hit the floor and exploded with a loud *whoosh*. Orange flames fanned wide on both sides, across the floor and up the walls, feeding on the fuel of the stinking gasoline.

When another bomb crashed into Tony's bedroom I dragged Jake in there. The size of the fire stunned me for a second and I threw away the safety blanket. It would feed this volatile mix. I picked up a homemade extinguisher.

"Pay attention," I said to Jake. "Push the paper wick back into the bottle. Put your finger over the hole and shake it like crazy!" The bottle fizzed wildly and I crouched. "Remember to get low." I blasted the fire with the foamy concoction and half of it died.

"We've got lots of these. Use 'em. I'll follow with the extinguisher and make sure they're totally out."

Linda dashed in from where she'd been watching in the doorway. She picked up a couple of Michael Specials. "They're bombing outside too," she said, and was gone.

"Cover your mouth," I yelled into the noise. I pulled my T-shirt up over my ears and clamped down on it with my teeth. The clinging smell of fire rose up with the heat of the flames. Putting out the inferno wiped every other thought out of my head.

Another cocktail landed on Tony's dresser and instantaneously the blaze covered the desk, the chair, and flashed up the wall. Electrical charges shot up my spine as I followed Jake, suffocating the dangerous patches of burning gasoline with the small extinguisher. A week ago this house had been my prison and now I wanted to save it.

As I emptied the last blanket of fire retardant on the desk flames, the fire suppression system in the ceiling activated. A shower of cold water soaked the room and soothed the heat on my face and arms. The Molotov cocktails had stopped raining down on us and I still had enough in the extinguisher to put out the last flame in the office. The sprinkler system would take the heat out of the scorched patches.

Across the hall we found Michael putting out one last firebomb. Smoke choked the air and he coughed as he blasted a layer of dry chemicals over a six-foot circle. When he'd checked our fire patches and we'd double-checked his, the three of us went out to the porch. Linda had single-handedly put out the worst of the fires there. Two were still smouldering but one flamed wildly. Michael took on the big one and Jake and I worked with Linda to finish off the two she'd managed to contain. From the corner of my eye, I saw a steady troop of looters carrying away cartons and cases from our basement. Strangers trampled the vegetable garden and ripped whole plants out of the ground.

The fires were under control so I shouted, "Michael, I'm going to lock the security doors," above the din of the extinguisher and the people surging through our yard.

"Be careful," he answered.

I ran inside and listened at the top of the stairs. Someone was already in my room. Things were being dumped on the floor. Before I tackled that problem, I slid the external security door shut in the kitchen and closed the fireproof shutters on the remaining windows. Then I clamped a lid on my nerves and went downstairs.

I peered around the corner at two girls, middle-school age, who were dredging through my stuff. One of them held up a pair of my briefs and giggled.

"What the hell?"

The girls dropped my clothes and looked at me, terrified.

"Mom said to find something to wear," the smaller one said. They were filthy, their hair matted and their clothes ripped in several places. They looked more like orphans than kids following mom's orders.

"You won't find anything in your size in my room. Didn't you see all the boxes of clothes beside the washer?"

"None left," said the littlest one and tears rolled down her waifish face.

"Here—take these." I snatched a handful of tank tops and tees out of the heap beside my desk. You can wear them as dresses. Take a couple more, for your mom." I realized I had no idea what size their mother might be. I saw the T-shirt Lexy had given me, with the sparkly dove flying over the word *peace*. "Take this one too—it'll fit most women."

They jerked the clothes out of my hands and ran down the short hallway to the storage part of the basement. As they disappeared, I saw a man emerge from the cellar with a case of water on his shoulder. He called to someone behind him, "Looks like there's more good stuff down the hall." He pointed to where I stood.

A woman walked up behind him, straining under the weight of a carton of canned kidney beans. The bottom of the barrel. Who'd take kidney beans if they could have tins of organic soup or spaghetti? The woman's dirty glasses glinted. "What's in there?" she said and took a step toward me.

As an answer, I slammed the internal security door between that part of the basement and the bedrooms. I pushed the metal bolts into place. *Thank you, Tony.* I whispered. His paranoia meant I still had a bedroom. I still had most of my clothes. I still had a refuge.

I wanted to slip into silence, into paralysis but I shook myself out of the darkness. After going from room to room and closing all the security grills on the rest of the basement windows, I walked upstairs on wobbly legs. Inside Tony's office, I shut off the fire suppression system and turned off the power to the fence.

"Sectors two and three are secure," I said to Michael. "The fence is cold and the sprinkler system is shutting down."

He grunted and sat down on the rocking chair. Slightly charred around the edges, it had survived. Beside it, the plastic loveseat squatted in a melted parody of its former self. Michael's eyes were the brightest they had been in days. The adrenaline rush had burned away his sleepiness.

I walked around the porch and hovered my hand over the scorched patches, testing for heat and finding none. At the end of the street the Green Death trucks were leaving, convoy style. The pedestrian crowd drifted away in fragments, weighed down by supplies that had taken years to accumulate. A dozen or so people still filed out of the basement with cases of basic food or flats of water under their arms. The two little girls followed the woman with the kidney beans. The three of them navigated their way, barefoot, around the broken glass in our yard. The man who said there was more good stuff in our bedrooms glared up at me and flipped the bird. In spite of my pounding heart, I smiled at him.

"I think we got it all." Linda came around from the other side of the porch. She clutched one last homemade extinguisher so hard I thought it might burst in her hands. Jake reached for it and prised her fingers off it. She put her head on his chest and he patted her hair.

"What a mess," I shook my head at the shattered glass and the fire-damaged timber of the porch. I turned my back on the busted windows and the view of the fire-retardant and water-soaked living room and bedroom. The sprinkler system spluttered to a final stop. I leaned against the doorjamb. Jake stepped away from his mother, locked his hands behind his back and started pacing.

As my desperation faded, shame took its place.

If we had trusted a little more, shared a bit when we still had the ability to do something, maybe none of this would have happened. People mightn't have joined the mob; they might have helped protect the place.

"Are you okay, Rowan?" Jake nodded at my hands. Mine were just like his, just like Michael's and just like Linda's, blackened and even singed in places.

"Gloves would've been nice," I said.

"And face masks," Michael added.

"The good thing is the house didn't burn down," Linda said. She stood by the railing, and gazed into the trashed yard.

"No it didn't," I said. "We still have a roof over our head, propane to run the generator and some fresh water in the underground tank."

She hunched her neck, maybe because she was the one who gave the Redgraves the map to the hidden treasure. White-hot resentment flared for a minute and then I let it go. I'd been too angry for too long and it hadn't done any good. Linda didn't intentionally hurt us. She simply trusted her neighbours. Only she picked the wrong ones to trust. When we needed her, she'd put her shoulder to the wheel with the rest of us. Now she clung on to the porch railing weakly, as if someone had sucked the life force out of her. In her short time in charge, she had failed colossally. Nothing I said could make her feel any worse.

Just like the earthquake had changed our lives in a few, ruinous moments, the mob had altered it even more. Our safety net was gone. With so little left to protect, Michael and I didn't have to stay home and do shifts any longer. In losing so much, we had gained something. We were normal now, the new normal. We were like everyone else. Free of the past and able to forge ahead.

As if he sensed my thoughts, Jake tapped Linda on the arm. "It's later," he said. "I want to know who my real father is. Right now."

CHAPTER 27 | FAMILY SECRETS AND THE NEW ORDER

NORTH VANCOUVER

Linda rubbed her neck, leaving a track of sooty fingerprints. "Phil Patterson is your father. In everything but blood. He's loved you and cared for you since you were a toddler."

"You're not answering my question." Jake thrust his chest out.

Linda dropped her chin. "Ray Sewchuk is your father."

"Who the hell is he?"

Linda didn't answer.

"Better known as Greg Phillips," I said softly.

"What?" Michael curled his lip as if maybe I'd invented the whole thing.

"I heard them talking on the porch last night," I said.

Linda sighed. "I'm sorry, Jacob. I was trying to protect you."

"From what? I'm sixteen. When were you going to tell me? I'm done with you trying to protect me from everything. Are you ever going to let live my own life?"

As he stepped toward her, Linda's entire body shook. Her voice broke when she tried to speak. "I just didn't know, Jacob. I just wasn't sure if you'd ever be ready."

"Why? Did you think it would kill me or something? Did you think I'd leave home and go searching for him?"

"I didn't think anything. Not really. Then I hadn't told you for so long, I hoped maybe I'd never *need* to tell you."

Jake threw his hands in the air and said, "Need to tell me? Are you freaking crazy?" His anger and frustration electrified the air. His body tensed as if he might lash out.

"Jake," I stamped my foot. "She's your mom. Don't forget that. No one will ever love you like she does." Then I burst into tears and ducked into the house. I ran downstairs and curled up on the corner of my bed.

"Hey." Michael knocked on the door.

"Go away," I said.

"No." He opened the door, checked I was dressed, and slipped inside. Sitting on the edge of my desk he said, "I've been waiting for you to come home. How's Tony?"

I covered my face with my hands. I didn't know where to start.

"His ring!" Michael said in a hoarse whisper.

I slid my hands down and looked at it as if it had just appeared on my thumb. "I don't want to say it," I whispered.

"Say what?" Michael's voice broke a little boy's. "Please, Rowan, you gotta tell me."

I got up and put my hands on his shoulders. "Tony's dead."

At those words we both started crying. I sobbed through the story of what had happened at the hospital. We cried and hugged each other. Finally we pulled apart and he leaned against the desk again as if it were the only thing holding him up. I crumpled back onto the bed. We stayed that way, numb and lost for words, letting the tick of my clock fill the raw silence. When my tears dried, I blew my nose one last time and announced, "It's time to find Mom."

Michael didn't say yes or no. He didn't have to. For the first time in years, words weren't necessary. Our own, unspoken language was back. He went to his room and I took a shower. I had to wash off the smell of this horrible, awful day.

Showered and changed, with the cash from the safe tucked into our pockets, Michael and I went upstairs. Jake and Linda sat on opposite sides of the kitchen table, their faces battle worn. An origami swan sat in the space between them, facing Linda.

The acrid smell of fire filled our house now, a reminder of all we'd lost. Michael took a loaf of bread out of the freezer and started making peanut butter sandwiches. I sat beside Jake and he gently pushed his shoulder into mine. "Mom and I are friends again," he said.

"That's good," I nodded. "You want to stay friends with your mom."

I waited for the right moment and ran my fingertips over the polished wooden surface of the kitchen table. I picked words and discarded them before I blurted out, "Tony died last night. In the hospital, in the one place I thought he would be safe."

Jake put his arm around me and I almost started crying again but I held on. I'd keep my pain as private as possible. Linda leaned across the table and stroked my hand, "Rowan, I'm so sorry."

"We're going to find Mom now," Michael said and licked the peanut butter knife clean. "You should be safe here, even without us. There's nothing left to steal really, is there?"

I added, "We're going to check every shelter and evacuation site and then start again if we have to."

Linda got up and hugged Michael before going into the pantry. She came out with a handful of chocolate bars. "I hid all the chocolate when I found it," she said. "If you want more, it's under all those bags of dog food." She dropped four into the pack that Michael was loading. "Take them for strength," she said. Then she handed the one to Jake. "I think this stuff is poison but some people don't mind it."

Michael and I pulled our full packs over our shoulders and stepped outside. A lump burned in my throat when I saw the devastation around us. Small wisps of smoke still drifted up from the singed porch and something rose from deep inside me and left with it. A new understanding dawned in its place.

Tony's fortress walls had not given him the independence he craved. A green Kawasaki would have set me free only until my money ran out. When Jake learned who his natural father was, sure it broke his mother's stranglehold on him, but the truth only trapped him in a web of more questions and riddles.

We were all wrong. Freedom was something inside us. It came from moving forward with a strong heart, no matter what life threw our way. Like texting a goodbye, even knowing you might not be around when the message is finally received.

Because the curfew was no longer in effect during daytime hours, the streets of North Van were flooded with a new type of energy. Pedestrians milled around the sidewalks and cars clogged the passable routes. People on foot looked at passing vehicles with anxious eyes, the way dazed victims look at invading armies. On Mountain Highway a slow parade of traffic moved bumper-to-bumper over the rough patches and around one big sinkhole. Drivers' faces were pinched tight. Michael eased Tony's truck into the line.

Crossing Burrard Inlet back to Vancouver, something I had done a million times in my life, now seemed like an epic challenge. The Ironworkers' Memorial Bridge that had opened that morning was closed again due to an accident. Police posted at the bottom of Mountain Highway were re-routing traffic. The cop who spoke to us told us to go home and wait for the phones to come on. Service was supposed be restored today for sure.

Ignoring that advice, we joined the slow crawl across the Lions Gate Bridge and arrived in Vancouver. We stopped at an evacuation centre in a West End high school but Mom wasn't there. She wasn't in any of the centres from downtown all the way out to the university. We drove home, to Mom's house, but the entire building was flattened. There was no note or other indication she'd been there. Gas was getting low so we decided to eat and think of a new plan.

As we were finishing the last of the sandwiches, my phone rang.

"Mom." I hit the speaker button.

"In case we get cut off—where are you?" Her voice never sounded better.

"Kitsilano, at our house. What was our house," Michael said. "The place is totalled. We've been looking for you. Are you okay?"

"I'm in the field hospital in McManus Stadium but they need my bed. How's Tony's place? Are you still staying there? Have you got room for me? Would he lose it if I came?"

"Tony's house is a rock," I said and it was true. A wet, singed, windowless rock. Still, way better than the evacuation centres we'd seen. "Of course we have room for you. Always. Don't worry about Tony."

"Traffic isn't moving fast but we're on our way," Michael said.

"What're you driving?"

"Tony's pickup. Lots of room." My voice sounded giddy.

"Come to the Marine Boulevard, Entrance G. I'll be waiting."

"We'll be there as soon as we can." The engine of the truck roared to life and we were on our way.

CHAPTER 28 | FORGING NEW ROADS

VANCOUVER, DOWNTOWN

An eternity later, as the gas indicator dipped toward empty, we arrived at McManus Stadium. Dozens of people buzzed around outside Entrance G. Many were injured and bandaged. The doors were wide open and we could see right into the underbelly of the stadium. Tables were lined up in rows. Tired looking people stared at computers on one side. People vied for attention on the other. Behind them more corridors branched out. Tables and chairs were set up out front. Patients, some with intravenous poles at their side, and visitors sat around them.

"There she is," Michael shouted and ran to a shady spot beside a parked ambulance. I blinked and chased after him. Mom was in a wheelchair wearing an ugly brown T-shirt.

I sank to my knees beside her. Michael and I hugged her from the sides of her chair. For a minute we all cried and laughed and said each other's names over and over. She stroked our faces and kissed the tops of our heads. When I stood up, I noticed a bruised bald spot shone on the back of her skull. Deep lines furrowed her face and dark rings circled her eyes.

Michael said, "How about we get you in the truck and go home?"

Worry ghosted across her face. "Everything's going to be okay." She cleared her throat. "But there is one thing you need to know."

I forced myself to look at the ragged blanket that covered her lap and legs. I didn't want to believe what I saw. Through a layer of chalk I whispered, "Mom?"

She rubbed her temples and sighed.

"Mom?" Michael echoed.

"My leg was crushed in the quake. I was pinned to the ground under a collapsed building." She smiled apologetically, as if she had disappointed us in some major way. "I'm afraid I'm going to need the chair for a while."

Michael swallowed and rested a hand on her shoulder. "You're alive and we're a family. That's what matters. We'll take care of you. Right, Rowan?"

"Yes. Of course yes." After everything we'd been through, I knew we could do it. A smile warmed me as I realized it was true. Life had changed and I'd learned to cope, to be resourceful, and to make good decisions. If Tony could be there, he'd be listening to me. He'd hear my voice and know I could and would do what needed to be done.

I climbed into the back of the king cab and watched as Mom hung onto Michael's arm. When she lurched out of the wheelchair Michael helped her balance and lift herself into the truck, I studied her movements for clues about her flexibility and strength. I was ready to be there when she needed me.

Stop. Think. Observe. Plan. Mom wouldn't get wound botulism because Michael and I wouldn't let that happen. She'd need fresh bandages, antiseptic, maybe even antibiotics. A list a mile long went through my head. It didn't matter how hard it would be go get everything we needed, we would.

As we drove home at a snail's pace I told Mom that Tony had died. She reached her hand back to me for comfort. "Kids,

I'm so sorry. He loved you both so much." Her words were strangled.

"No sympathy while I'm driving, please." Michael swiped at his mouth.

"Of course not." She shook herself and sat a little straighter. "He was so nervous about being a father, afraid that he wouldn't be good enough. But look at you two—you've turned out strong and smart and self-reliant. He was so proud. I'll miss him and his particular brand of crazy."

I swallowed the razor-sharp lump in my throat and said, "Well, we've had other things to distract us since we found out. Like the fact that the house was trashed and looted today."

"Oh no." She bit her lip.

I realized she'd left a place that was safe and dry to come to our burnt-out house in the suburbs so I rushed to reassure her. "We still have some food—everything that was in the kitchen and pantry. And we've got power and heat, plus lots of filtered drinking water which is way more than most people."

"I'd rather be with you two in a tent than any evacuation centre or field hospital," she said with a small smile.

NORTH VANCOUVER

We found a gas station with a large wooden sign out front. Hand-painted red letters a foot high declared *GAS TODAY*. Below that, in words we couldn't read until we almost drove over it, black letters said, *$10 a litre cash only.*

"That's robbery," Mom murmured.

"It's the only game in town so I'm guessing they can ask what they want." Michael stopped at the end of the shorter line-up for the pumps. I looked into the back of the dented old car beside us and saw something rare and precious. Unopened loaves of bread. I checked again. There were two of them. Beside the bread was a bag of potatoes, canned food, and packages of pasta.

I lowered my window and yelled, "Excuse me?"

A woman in large sunglasses turned her head and cracked her window an inch.

"Where'd you get the food?"

"Supply boats came in to Lynnterm today and handed out rations. They ran out a little while ago but promised there'll be more tomorrow." She closed her window.

Groceries meant a lot of things. It meant life was getting back to normal. I pulled back my shoulders. When we got to the front of the line and took the maximum gas allowed, twenty-five litres, I started to hum. We would survive.

Jake and Linda had started clean-up in our absence. They'd taken shovels from the garage and moved the broken glass to a corner of the yard. Bedding hung over the clothesline. Mattresses were leaned against the windows to dry out. The chickens were fine and Jake had collected all the eggs from the henhouse.

Greg arrived back in the early evening and helped us settle Mom into my room. He promised to bring more dressings and painkillers from the hospital. He even he knew a physiotherapist who might drop by.

The upstairs would take a few days to dry out and hours to scrape all the chemical retardant off the floors and furniture so Michael found air mattresses for Linda and Greg to sleep on until their rooms were ready again. Linda decided to sleep in the kitchen and Greg moved into the TV room in the basement. Mom took my bed and I got the trundle.

That night I dreamt about the Christmas when we got snowed in. We were at Mom's place. A fire crackled in the fireplace and Nana was alive again. I smelled her jasmine perfume. She told me to stir the pudding and make a wish.

"Tony." Mom's shrill voice crashed into my greeting card dream. "Help me," she begged.

My heart pounded. I crawled to the bed and turned on lamp. Tears poured down her face. "Mom, it's okay," I said and held her hand.

Her eyes were all messed up with fear and confusion. She peered at me for a minute before recognition calmed her. "Oh, Rowan," she sighed. "It was so awful. I was trapped under that building again. In the darkness. I was so alone."

"Please give me my bag," she said, her voice steady. I handed her up the ugly supermarket sack. She brought out a handful of pill bottles and lined them up on the night table. She opened one, shook out two pills and swallowed them with half a glass of water.

"That'll get me through the night." She smiled. I kissed her and turned off the light. Then I opened the blind and let the moonlight in so I could watch until the tightness around her mouth softened. When I slipped back into my bed Misty joined me.

I was almost asleep when Mom whimpered again, "Help me."

I waited, rigid and worried, for more. All night long she muttered those words over and over. It was weird because she didn't seem to wake up. I tried to sleep but mostly I lay there and listened. I even listened to the silence.

Think. Observe. Plan. I was strong and I was a survivor and I'd ride the future with these simple tools. Suddenly I caught my breath. I was strong and a survivor because Tony had made me that way. He left me that gift.

EPILOGUE

The first dog shelter we checked was the one I'd seen at 15th and Grand Boulevard. They had dozens of dogs but Oliver wasn't one of them. I slumped against the window as Michael drove across town to SeyLynn Park.

A woman sat outside a tent, on a folding camping chair, with her back turned to the rest of the world. When she saw the bag of dog food we'd brought she laughed and her short blond braids bounced like exclamation marks. "I've been sitting here wondering how we were going to feed the pack tonight. You must have heard my prayers."

"I hope you heard mine," I said and showed her the picture of Oliver.

"He may be in there but I've lost track. We get one dog back to its owners and five more strays take its place."

"Do you want this here? Or would that be bear bait?" Jake asked as he set the bag of food on the ground. "Is there somewhere safe to keep it?"

The woman dug into the pocket of her shorts and brought out a key with a VW logo. "See the Jetta at the edge of the parking lot? The one with the tree across it? That's our car. We stopped to walk our dogs and we've been stuck here ever since. The trunk is still accessible. Could you put it in there?"

I glanced toward the dogs.

"Go check." Her fingers were soft on my elbow as she nudged me toward the tennis court.

Michael and Jake hauled the dog food over to the crushed car and I walked toward the makeshift kennel. A couple of baby baths were set up as drinking bowls. A beagle stood in the middle of one, drinking and cooling down at the same time. When it saw me approaching, it bayed mournfully but no other dog stirred. Most were crowded in the only available shade, a shadow cast by blankets tied over the corner of the court. The dogs all seemed a bit thin and a few lay lethargically in the full sun. I strained to see a certain white terrier mix but it was impossible to pick out a single dog in that sea of fur and dust. A few animals lifted their heads as I neared their chain-link walls but most seemed indifferent to the parade of humans outside their jail.

I stood for a few minutes, not wanting to go any farther. *What if Oliver wasn't inside? What if he was dead and all my searching was pointless?* I let worry rattle me one more time before I folded the black blanket and put it into the wooden box.

Jake looked over at me from beside the VW. He gave me a thumbs' up and smiled. That gesture was the push I needed. I flicked my bangs off my face and moved to the entrance of the court. I squinted at the mess of dogs in there. Then I cleared my throat and called, in a high-pitched voice, "Oliver! *Olly-Olly-Olly-Oliver*! I've got treats."

In the farthest corner a small white head popped up. Wiry brown hair circled the left eye. I called again, not trusting my eyes. In a single leap Oliver cleared the pile of sleeping dogs. He flew toward me, his feet a blur.

ACKNOWLEDGEMENTS

There are writers who sit in busy rooms and turn out word-perfect novels. I am not one of them. From its first rough draft in 2010 to its final form, *Lockdown* went through countless versions with the help of many people.

First of all, a big thank you to my husband, Alan Bolitho, who listened as I read the entire manuscript aloud—not once but three or four times. In spite of not being a fiction reader, he offered intelligent, good-humoured suggestions. More than just a great partner at first aid and emergency preparedness courses both in Canada and Australia, he assisted with technical aspects of the story.

Thank you to my enthusiastic, tireless writing partner, Allison Doke, who read each revision of every scene and always came back with thoughtful comments. Her encouragement kept me going when I might have lost faith.

Thank you to my wonderful editor, Anita Daher, whose confidence in me and this project, along with razor-sharp insights and help with structure, made the story shine. I learned so much from working with her and will be forever grateful. Thanks also to Great Plains Teen Fiction who took a chance on an emerging writer.

Years ago another author, the late V. M. Caldwell, encouraged me to turn my hand to writing. Her trust in my abilities never faltered. Val nudged me to this path and although I said thank you often, I wish she could have seen my first published novel.

ACKNOWLEDGEMENTS

Thank you to the amazing Alyssa Brugman, who believed in me when my skills were rough and untrained. Without her urging I might have stopped writing before I started. Thanks also for the openhearted generosity on many levels.

It took me a long time to seek out writing teachers and coaches and I thank them all: Kathy Page and Pearl Luke of Salt Spring Island, Bruce McAllister of California. I should have found you sooner.

To the people who read an early draft and helped pinpoint what did and didn't work—my beta readers, Lynn Crymble, Bix Watson, Sophie Watson, and Megan Dodd—thank you.

Oceans of gratitude are owed to the Community Fire Units (Fire & Rescue, NSW), North Shore Emergency Management Office and St. John Ambulance for their fine work in the community, as well as Dorit Mason and her expertise.

Thank you also to my sister, Victoria Anderson, who listened without interrupting and was there for my journey. This work also benefited from the support of the North Shore Writers' Association and others whose fellowship broke the isolation of the writing caper. If your name should be here and isn't, I apologize. Sometimes it's hard to remember all my blessings.